MW01125287

BILLIONAIRE'S CHRISTMAS

BY
SIERRA CARTWRIGHT

BILLIONAIRE'S CHRISTMAS
Copyright © 2018 Sierra Cartwright
First Print Publication: November 2018
Editor: Nicki Richards, What's Your Story Editorial Services
Line Editing by Jennifer Barker
Proofing by Bev Albin, ELF
Layout Design by BB eBooks
Cover Design by Rachel Connolly
Photographer: Wander Aguiar
Cover Model: Thom Panto
Photo provided by ©Wander Book Club
Promotion by Once Upon An Alpha, Shannon Hunt

All rights reserved. Except for use in a review, no part of this publication
may be reproduced, distributed, or transmitted in any form, or by any
means, electronic or mechanical, including photocopying, recording, or by
any information storage and retrieval system, without prior written
permission of the author.

This is a work of fiction. Names, characters, places, brands, media, and
incidents are either the products of the author's imagination or are used
fictitiously, and any resemblance to any actual persons, living or dead, is
entirely coincidental.

The author acknowledges the trademarked status and trademark owners of
various products referenced in this work of fiction. The publication/use of
these trademarks is not authorized, associated with, or sponsored by the
trademark owners.

Adult Reading Material

Disclaimer: This work of fiction is for mature (18+) audiences only and
contains strong sexual content and situations.

It is a standalone with my guarantee of satisfying, happily ever after.

All rights reserved.

DEDICATION

A very special thank you to Sierra's Super Stars. You are the best reader group ever! I appreciate you.

Shannon, you are amazing. Simply amazing.

For Whit and Nicki, the Titans world wouldn't exist without you.

Always, I want to thank my other key teammates, Bev, Jen, ELF, the All Star Beta Readers, and Rachel. Thank you!

CHAPTER ONE

"Are you ready?" Rafe asked.

The sound of her fiancé's richly timbred voice slammed Hope's pulse into hyperdrive. She turned to see him leaning a shoulder against the doorjamb that separated the bedroom from the bathroom. He swept his gaze over her as if she were a treasured prize.

"Jesus." As if unable to stop himself, he took a few steps toward her. "You're exquisite."

His approval was her aphrodisiac, making her knees bend.

"Show me." He made a circle with his index finger, and she twirled around.

The dark-green floor-length gown flared as she spun, thanks to the A-line and the daring slit up the front. The dress had double V necklines with draped pleats wrapping the bodice.

"What do you think of it?" he asked when she stopped in front of him.

"I love it." The dress was elegant as well as risqué. Rafe had custom ordered it for her, and he'd had a hand in the design. "It's everything I dared hope."

He crooked his finger, beckoning her toward him.

Her pulse raced and her stilettoes echoed on the tile floor. It didn't matter that she and Rafe had been together eight months. When her lover, her Dom, gave an instruction, every feminine instinct responded with a flood of pheromones.

"You look like a princess, my sweet, sweet Hope."

"And you look like…" Words failed her. He wore a black tuxedo with a snowy-white shirt, elegant forest-green cummerbund, and matching bow tie. Rafe always dressed well, but this evening, he was so devastatingly handsome that he sucked the oxygen from the room. With a grin, she settled on, "A Titan."

Heir to the legendary Sterling Worldwide hotel empire, Rafe was descended from a long, successful line of men, including one who had helped found the Zetas, a secret society. Tonight was the group's Christmas party and semiannual induction of new members.

"And today you become one of us."

Her tummy jumped. The waiting list to join was years long, but because Celeste—Hope's mentor and a member of the steering committee—had sponsored her, Hope's approval had been pushed through in record time.

"I have a gift for you," he said.

Innuendo laced his words. The thrill that rocked her, heated her, chilled her when he gave her orders was like a drug. If she went without too long, she needed a fix.

"Oh, I have a *special* gift for you as well," he added. "But that will need to wait until we return."

He took her hand and guided her into the bedroom of their rented Magnolia Cottage on the grounds of the Parthenon—the society's Louisiana plantation. Many times when he visited, he stayed in a room in the original home, now called the Grand House. But since they'd become a couple, he preferred the extra space and privacy of the one-bedroom accommodation. On top of the dresser lay a large box. "Open it," he encouraged.

A white-gold choker with a dozen strands of tiny diamonds lay nestled in velvet, reflecting light everywhere. Stunned, she glanced at him.

"What do you think?"

It wasn't a collar. For now, he didn't require her to wear one every day. But there was no doubt about his intention. "It's...beautiful."

"May I?" He held out his hand, and she picked up the piece of jewelry and placed it across his palm.

Until Rafe, she'd known almost nothing about BDSM, and he'd taught her that each relationship was unique. What she shared with him was as much emotional as physical. His constant mindfucks created an unbreakable bond.

Responding to the unspoken command in his turbulent blue eyes, she turned and lifted her hair, baring her nape to him.

Since his fingers were so big, it took him several attempts to fasten the necklace. "You need a ladies' maid," he said.

"But then I wouldn't have your hands on me."

He leaned forward to kiss that sensitive area on the back of her neck.

"We could skip the event," she said.

"But we won't. Waiting makes you all the more responsive later."

"Waiting annoys me," she corrected, despite the fact he was right, and they both knew it.

"When you're pissy with me, your eyes take on more of a golden hue. It's easy to imagine you as a spitfire or satyr."

"You're impossible, Mr. Sterling." Before they were intimate, she'd confessed that orgasm denial intrigued her. Edging, he'd called it, and making her wait to come had ended up being a major turn-on for him. He'd told her he loved her whimpers, and her frantic pleas for relief. By the time he relented, granting her permission to come, her climax would destroy her. As much as she liked the stunning orgasms, there were times she'd regretted being so honest with him.

"You may put down your hair."

Once she did, Rafe gripped her shoulders, his large hands warm on her bare skin.

"I'm so fucking proud you're mine." He turned her to look at him, and his gaze lingered on the jewelry he'd fastened into place. Rafe fed his fingers into her hair, made a fist, then pulled back her head. "I can't wait to show you off."

She swallowed. On their first trip to Louisiana, he'd taken her to Vieille Rivière, a private restaurant outside of New Orleans. He'd dressed her in a scandalous outfit. Her nerves had been strung tight as they walked through the dining room and she'd seen Doms with subs, some kneeling, others wearing far less than she had been. Though she hadn't been comfortable being exposed, Hope had enjoyed the experience more than she thought she might.

On this trip to Louisiana, he'd said he wanted to take her to the Quarter, a BDSM club he frequented before their relationship began.

So far, she hadn't found the courage to agree. Her refusals created tension in their relationship. To her, going to the Quarter meant she'd be on public display. And more, she would be vulnerable in front of others. But she hid her deepest fear from him…that she wouldn't measure up to the submissives there. They were experienced and composed, while she was a novice, more awkward than elegant.

"I love you, Hope." Intent radiated through his eyes, and instant arousal spilled through her.

Rafe didn't have to ask her to open her mouth—she did so without hesitation. He didn't so much kiss her as mark her, devouring her, simulating an indecent sex act. With his tongue, he fucked her mouth, seeking confirmation that she knew they belonged together.

She ached to have him finger her heated pussy. "Please…"

Surprising her, he grabbed the skirt of her gown and hiked it up, mindless of the extravagant cost of the material.

Because he liked it, she was naked beneath. She never knew when he'd want access to her, and being slowed down by underwear aggravated him. On one occasion, to show his displeasure, he'd kept her thong damp for an entire evening, then refused her an orgasm, even after requiring her to suck him off. She'd learned her lesson.

He slid a finger between her labia. Her clit was already swollen, and a moan ripped from her throat.

"You're perfect. *We* are perfect." His eyes darkened. "Spread your legs." He teased her needy entrance. "Wider."

"Yes, Sir…" Since he was still kissing her, the word was more in her imagination than anything, but he knew, *knew* what she wanted.

As he ended the kiss, he fed more of his finger inside her. "One day, we're going to make a baby."

"Rafe…" He knew when she was the most vulnerable to him. She wanted that also.

"Twins might be nice," he said, now finger-fucking her.

"Twins?" Shocked, she met his eyes. Most of the time she could read him, but right now she couldn't. She had no idea whether he was teasing or not. He both terrified and excited her. "Are there twins on either side of your family?"

"No."

She exhaled. "There aren't on my side either. So that's not going to happen." Thank God. One tiny dictatorial Rafe would be enough to handle.

He slipped a second finger inside her. His rough tenderness made it impossible to think. She surrendered to him and the magic of the moment, of dreams coming true, of a crisp Christmas season near New Orleans.

"We should start trying," he said. "I understand it can take a while to conceive. And I'm going to enjoy the hell out of every moment of trying."

Her insides clutched, from the spell of his words as well as what he was doing to her body. He parted her farther, inserting a third finger into her, something he'd never done before. She couldn't fill her lungs. Desperately, she grabbed his lapels to hold herself up. "I'm on birth control."

"Which you can stop anytime." His smile was wicked. "Tonight even."

What would it be like, to have nothing standing in the way? "I think we should be married first." In the light, her yellow diamond winked. For her stunning engagement ring, he'd splurged on a massive rectangular-shaped center stone, saying it reminded him of her eyes. He'd added two smaller diamonds on each side, and the contrast of the white and bright yellow turned heads, including hers. At times she wanted to pinch herself to be sure their relationship was real.

"We should arrange that," he said.

Her body clenched around his hand as he changed his angle to press a finger against her G-spot. *Holy heavens.*

"When?"

She shook her head to clear it. "When...what?"

"The wedding date?" he prompted.

"You're taking unfair advantage."

"I prefer to think of it as a tactical, strategic offensive." Notching his fingers apart, he grinned.

"Rafe!" Lost, she squirmed. He seized the opportunity to drive deeper, making her mad with desire. "I need...!"

He eased back a little, allowing her to exhale, then captured her mouth as he bore forward.

God.

He fucked her with his hand, sought more. And because she wanted all the same things that he did, she capitulated when he ended the kiss. "August."

"August?"

"I need time to plan."

"I could have it arranged in twenty minutes. We can be married at the atrium rooftop."

He was referring to one of the most spectacular places in all of Houston—at a property he owned. She'd gone to an event with him there before, and she'd fallen in love with it.

"The catering department will handle it all. We can have pictures during the day, the ceremony at sunset, dancing beneath the stars."

Even while he continued his relentless sensual assault on her all too willing body, Hope envisioned the picture he painted. She knew how magical it could be with lights on the potted trees, and if the evening was nice enough, the rooftop could be opened. "I need a dress."

"Simple."

"You're impossible."

"It takes seventy-two hours for a license. We could be married before the New Year, which is my preference." He pressed against her G-spot again. "I'm willing to wait until spring. May at the latest," he compromised.

"Fine." He'd won. Once again, the formidable Rafe

Sterling had outmaneuvered her. Hope was willing to bet he'd planned on a ceremony in late spring all along, but he'd orchestrated this seduction, suggesting they tie the knot before the New Year, just so that she would agree to May.

He leaned in closer, until they breathed the same air. His masculine scent stamped her.

And then it hit her—they'd set a date. They were getting married. Really getting married. "We're going to do this?"

"Oh yes. You're going to be my bride. This is the second happiest day of my life."

"Second?"

"The first was when you said yes to my proposal."

As he moved his fingers in her, remaining upright was becoming more and more difficult. The need for orgasm clawed at her, but because of his careful manipulations, he ensured she couldn't get off. "Rafe... May I...?"

"Should I leave you like this, your sex wide open, your arousal dripping down your thighs during dinner? While we dance?"

The idea excited her. She wanted to come, but if she didn't, she would ache all night, be focused on him, thirsty for the tanginess of his cock. She'd experience the aftereffects of his penetration for hours.

"Tell me what you want."

She couldn't believe she was going to say it, and she knew she would regret it the moment the words left her mouth, but the thrill drew her in a way nothing else could. "Edge me, Sir." This, she could give him.

"Fuck…" He flattened his thumb against her clit, the pressure causing a tiny mind-blowing ache that made her whimper.

Then he thrust in an out several times until she was crying. The buildup inside her was unbearable.

"That will have to do you until tonight, when I properly reward your sacrifice and courage." He pulled out his hand. If he hadn't wrapped an arm around her for support, she would have toppled over. He glanced at his watch. "It's almost time for us to leave. Are you ready?"

She nodded. He led her to the mattress, where she sank down to recover. After washing his hands, he returned to the bedroom, checked his cuffs, then adjusted his bow tie in the mirror.

He offered his arm, and she stood on still-shaky legs. Her thighs were sticky from her essence, and her pussy was damp. She knew he wouldn't grant permission to clean herself up, so she didn't bother asking. In a moment of naughty insight, she realized she liked knowing that under her gorgeous gown, she bore traces of his dominance.

Near the door, she picked up her clutch. Then she

caught sight of herself in a small mirror. In horror, she gasped. He'd kissed off her lipstick. Her hair was mussed, as if she'd just left their bed. There was a tiny smear of mascara next to one eye. "I'm a wreck."

"In the most delightful way, yes."

"You were going to let me go out like this?"

"Without a second thought."

"Everyone will know…"

"Know what?" He grinned. "That I am the most fortunate man on the planet?"

She pushed away his arm. "You'll need to give me a couple of minutes."

"If you take too much time, your arousal will abate, and I'll have no choice but to take you to the brink again."

Hope gaped at him. She knew he wasn't kidding. He'd risk being late to the festivities in order to make her fantasies come true. She dashed into the bathroom, as fast as she could on the peep-toe heels that he loved so much.

At a casual pace, he followed her, leaning against the doorjamb as he watched her.

"Making sure I behave, Mr. Sterling?"

"I'd hate to have to punish you for wiping your pussy."

How long do we have to stay at the event?

She did her best to tame her hair. She dabbed the

stray mascara from her skin and reapplied a fresh coat. Then she swiped on a layer of lipstick.

In the mirror, she met his gaze.

He was focused on her, his cock swollen against the zipper of his tailored trousers.

"I suggest you finish up. Otherwise I have another use for your mouth."

She was tempted to stall. But an entire evening awaited them. "Yes, Sir."

He adjusted his cock.

Hope pushed the lipstick cover back on, then dropped the tube into her bag and fastened the clasp. Then she inhaled to cover her nerves. "I'm ready."

CHAPTER TWO

Wind gusted from the north, making the mid-December night damp and cold. He draped a wrap around her shoulders before extending his elbow for support as they walked toward the car.

Within minutes, he turned onto the half-circle driveway, and the mansion—called the Great House by members—came into view. Hope gasped. The building was always imposing, but decorated for Christmas, it was stunning.

The porch, second-story gallery, and the ten Grecian pillars had been wrapped with twinkling white lights in honor of the holidays. Wreaths were hung in the windows, and garland draped the door.

Tonight, a valet stand had been set up in front of the staircase. Even though an attendant opened her door, she waited for Rafe to assist her from the car. Every day, in dozens of ways, he made her feel cherished.

Arm in arm, they climbed the stairs, and both sets of

elegant double doors were opened for them.

The lobby was always spectacular. Tonight, with its mechanical moving reindeer and a twenty-foot Christmas tree filling the air with the fresh scent of pine, it was amazing. Both curved staircases leading to the second floor were wrapped with greenery and lights. At the top, in the middle, was a platform, in the shape of a semicircle. The Zeta society's symbol, a lowercase Greek *z*, adored the wood.

"Evening, Rafe."

Stunned, Hope froze as Eldon Misken joined them. The entrepreneur had never completed college, yet he spent his days trying to solve the world's problems, launching rockets, manufacturing stylish, electric cars, harnessing the power of the sun and wind. Some people called him a visionary. Others considered him a narcissistic crackpot. After a moment of gawking, Hope forced herself to close her mouth. A quick look at his right hand confirmed he was wearing a Zeta ring, not that she was surprised. Because of privacy rules, she hadn't seen a membership roster. After tonight, she'd be able to log in to the Zeta's website to find the information herself.

"Eldon," Rafe said, and the two men exchanged handshakes. "May I introduce my bride-to-be, Hope Malloy."

"Congratulations, Ms. Malloy," he said. "I understand you're going to become a member tonight?"

"I am."

"Double congratulations, then. On the wedding and on being accepted into the Zetas." He shook Hope's hand.

She wished it wasn't gauche to request an autograph. One of her matchmakers, Skyler, was a huge Eldon fan, and it would make a heck of a Christmas present for her.

"I need to spend a few days in DC," Eldon said. "There's some doubters on Capitol Hill who need their hands shaken. Some of this progress ruffles the feathers of their constituents." He said it with a note of disdain, as if there was nothing he detested more.

"Will you be staying at The Sterling Parkland?"

Rafe is more than a passing acquaintance with Eldon?

"My admin tells me it's fully booked."

How was it possible that billionaires had problems getting hotel reservations?

"Would you like a White House view?"

"Lafayette Park, so the scenery will encourage me to get out for a run."

"Send me the dates and I'll take care of it. Enjoy your evening," Rafe said as they parted ways.

"Wait," she said, the moment the man was out of earshot. "You know Eldon? As in, you're friends?"

"After all this time, I've managed to impress you?" He grinned. "I would have introduced you earlier."

"I want his autograph."

"What?"

"Tell him that's part of the deal."

Rafe stopped walking to stare at her.

"Skyler has a crush on him."

"You're serious about this."

She smiled her appreciation. "You're the greatest, Mr. Sterling."

"Because I can get you a signature?"

"Well, it is just one of your impressive talents…" She adjusted his bow tie, and his eyes lit up in response, in promise.

Waitstaff garbed in tuxedoes—even the women—threaded their way through the room, serving appetizers. Several bartenders were mixing custom cocktails. One muddled mint from the plantation's greenhouse. Throughout the room, a couple of other stations had been set up to serve wine, beer, and champagne.

"What can I get you?" Rafe asked.

"Champagne."

"Why did I bother asking? If you'll excuse me?"

"Thank you." Most times, when she attended society functions, she was working, talking to Houston's single women, adding business cards to her purse. But tonight, she was among two hundred guests, the elite from all over the world. No matter how she tried to pretend it was normal, she was a little unnerved. She was an imposter here, not born into wealth, and she hadn't made her mark on the world as an entrepreneur or rule changer, and she'd been bumped to the top of the years-long wait list.

She exhaled a thankful smile when Celeste walked—or more like glided—over. In addition to serving on the Society's steering committee, Celeste owned Fallon and Associates, a high-profile PR group. Or that's what their website proclaimed. The reality was far different. When media spin wasn't enough, the organization made problems go away. How far their reach went, Hope had no idea.

"Darling Hope!" Celeste kissed both of Hope's cheeks. "You're radiant."

Celeste's floor-length gold gown had thousands of beads sewn on her bodice. The back swept into a jaw-dropping train. She attracted the attention of everyone close enough to see her. "You look like you could rule the world."

"I intend to." Celeste laughed, more with conviction than mirth. "How are you faring at your first official Zeta Society event?"

"I feel as if I have fraud alert stamped on my fore-head."

"Don't. You earned your place here."

"With…" She glanced around. There was a former football player, a quarterback, if she wasn't mistaken. A poet laureate. An A-list actor, and across the room, his ex-wife who was now an ambassador. One of Texas's senators stood in the corner, with a crowd gathered around him. And Eldon Misken, for God's sake. "With all these Titans?"

"You, my dear, are matchmaker to some high profile individuals. You know their secrets and their—how shall we say it? Peccadillos? Knowing a person's secrets and keeping them, is powerful beyond compare."

Unable to help herself, Hope grinned. "Okay. I still may not belong, but I feel better about it."

"Don't fool yourself. You're a successful entrepreneur. Prestige is growing in reputation, which means you'll have worldwide clients before long. Not everyone here is a legacy member, and to be frank, we like it that way. We seek out unusual occupations. We wouldn't be as vibrant, as forward-thinking, solution oriented if we had the same old stodgy people admitted year after year."

"But the wait list…"

No one was close enough to overhear them, but Celeste leaned forward anyway and took one of Hope's hands. "It doesn't always go in order. Yes, we do consider application date, but there are always exceptions. Your membership is not without precedent, Hope. It does us good to have more women among our ranks. In terms of female representation, we have a lot of ground to make up. You did very well during your screening."

The process had been more than a little intimidating. Three months prior, she and Rafe had visited the Parthenon. For four hours, she'd sat in one of the boardrooms, behind a table facing all the members of the steering committee. They'd sat on a dais in comfortable padded chairs, while she'd been relegated to a wooden chair that wobbled each time she shifted. A light had been pointed at her, and they hadn't allowed for any breaks. After an hour, she'd gotten up and dragged over a more comfortable one from the corner of the room.

That was the only time that Celeste had smiled. And Hope had realized that taking action had been part of the test.

The interminable wait for a decision had been far more difficult, though. Rafe had said he had no doubts, but for weeks she'd checked email and messages like a woman obsessed.

"You wouldn't be here if you didn't deserve it," Celeste reiterated. "So, let this be the last you speak of it." She lifted a hand in front of her face to be certain they couldn't be overheard. "Some of these people desperately need your services. Like that gentleman over there." She indicated a man with rakishly good looks, wearing a tailored tuxedo. He'd added a splashy, interest-snagging cobalt-blue bowtie and cummerbund.

Hope shook her head. "I don't recognize him."

"Zane Kentwood."

Though Hope recognized the name, she couldn't place it.

"The prodigy who's been placed in charge of Bradford Capital Management."

"As in the hedge fund?"

Celeste smiled her approval. "I knew you'd keep up."

Hope's eyes widened as she took a second look at Zane. Bradford Capital was recognized as one of the top ten hedge funds in the world. If her memory was correct, they had over a hundred fifty billion dollars under management. They counted pension funds, university endowments, cities and towns, even central banks as clients. They existed for people with ridiculous amounts of money.

"The bigger the risk, the greater the chances that Bradford will be the firm of choice. Thanks to Zane. When he started interning, they had less than a third of that money. He challenged the founder on some key investment policies. Most people thought he'd get fired. Instead, he became Marvin's protégé." Then, angling her body conspiratorially, Celeste added, "He still lives in the same apartment he had in college. The man's far too much of a workaholic. It's time for someone to shake up his life. I think you should find the woman who's brave enough to do it."

Hope was cautious. "He should want a wife before we find him one."

Celeste shrugged, and Hope couldn't tell if it meant Celeste agreed or not.

"Well at least talk to Randy. Near the bar. The one stabbing his olive into his martini and considering drowning himself in the glass." She sighed. "Owns a chain of bridal stores—one in Houston, another in Dallas, one in San Antonio, and he's opening another in Austin. He needs a husband or at least a partner. He's going to die of loneliness."

"We've had a few requests for same-sex partners." Her male associate, Tony, had suggested they add that as a part of their business. "We might be able to help."

"And for God's sake, I need to get Remington Hagan in to see you."

She frowned. "Who's that?"

"He's black ops. Undercover stuff. Cloak-and-dagger, trying to keep the world safe from the bogeyman. Has something of a hero complex. That's not a clinical diagnosis—it's mine. His wife died in a plane crash about three years ago, and since then he's taken some stupid risks. It's time for him to move on."

More than many, Hope understood that not everyone could. Hope's father had been killed in action right around the time Hope was born. Her mother, Cynthia, had believed that they were soul mates, and she'd spent her life dedicated to taking care of veterans, even at the expense of spending time with Hope. "Some people never do."

"Remington needs to, for the sake of the world. Tell me you'll talk to him."

"You know that's not my business model." Prestige preferred to deal with people who'd decided on their own that they were ready to get married, for whatever reasons. They had clients who were in their late twenties, all the way up to a feisty octogenarian.

"Adapt and overcome." Celeste recited one of her mottos.

"Do you ever stop?"

"Everyone needs someone. I simply won't allow some other company to glom on to him and steal the commission from beneath your nose. You need to be more aggressive, Hope."

Rafe rejoined them. "Celeste! You're stunning as ever." He was carrying two glasses of champagne. After handing one to Hope, he offered the other to Celeste.

She accepted it with a "Thanks."

"Welcome to the Zeta Society," Celeste said, lifting her glass to Hope. "We have the world's elite as members." Then she rolled her eyes. "Except for that pesky damn senator from Texas. Annoying as hell in that ten-gallon hat. Who wears them anymore?" She waved a hand. "Rafe, we have *got* to find a good candidate to run against him so we can call him a *former* senator." Then, like an empress, Celeste floated away, train dragging behind her, people parting as she approached.

"She needs a crown," Hope said.

"I'd be surprised if she didn't have one," Rafe admitted. "Since I seem to have lost my champagne, I need to go back to the bar. Will you be okay by yourself?"

"Perhaps I'll go speak with Mr. Hagan. Celeste suggests he might be a possible client."

"Business always calls." He leaned toward her. His breath warm on her skin, he whispered into her ear, "Be thinking about who's going to fuck you senseless tonight."

With his simple, direct statement, he'd reminded her of what they'd started earlier, and heat crashed through her once again. He'd had that power over her since the very first time they met.

"I'll find you," he promised.

She took a sip of the excellent sparkling wine before making her way toward Remington.

"Ah." His smile was genuine, though touched with a brush of pain. If she hadn't been looking for it, she might have missed it. "Celeste told me she was going to sic a matchmaker on me."

"Ouch," she said with a smile.

"No offense meant, Ms. Malloy. I'm afraid Celeste is right that I've lost myself in my work." Perhaps because Hope was safe, someone he didn't know, not judgmental, he went on. "That's not the right word. Drowned myself in it. Better than other things, though?"

"I know how bad it hurts."

"Larissa has been gone three years. Sometimes it seems like yesterday and that I'll wake up from the nightmares. I listen to an old voicemail so I don't forget her voice." He stared into his glass. Vodka, if she wasn't mistaken. "With my job, we knew we were taking a risk that our time together would be short. But…" He shook his head. "I wasn't prepared for it. I don't know that I would have had the courage to ask her out if I'd known she would die before me."

At the raw emotion strung through his words, Hope's heart twisted.

"After the funeral, I realized how strong she'd been. She took a chance, lived with me being gone for weeks without any contact." He angled his head, and the light played on a faint scar that ran from his temple to his ear, then curved back into his close-cropped hair. "In her place, I would have been a coward."

"She sounds very special."

"Part of me thinks it would be better to remain alone, even if others don't think so."

"The holidays can be difficult."

"Tonight is a celebration. I didn't mean to spoil your evening." He smiled.

She marveled at the stunning transformation, from a man filled with pain to a charming companion, emotions locked up as if they weren't permitted to get in the way of the rest of his life. He was a chameleon of sorts—that no doubt made him great at his job.

"Congratulations are in order. Welcome to the Zetas."

"Thank you." Because he'd been so honest with her, she made her own confession. "It's a bit surreal."

"I agree with you."

"Really?"

"Connections are forged that last a lifetime. If you have the chance, be sure to attend the annual gathering, or as much of it as you can. I've missed a few years because of other…obligations, but I try to take my leave around that time."

"And the bonfire?" she asked.

He laughed. "Including togas and flat sandals."

Rafe had teased her the same way. "Foiled again." Years ago, she'd read an exposé written by a reporter who'd sneaked in to one of the Society's annual gatherings. He'd reported about mysterious dancing around the bonfire with some strange rituals and burning effigies that she suspected were more folklore than fact, but she couldn't find anyone to confirm or deny it. "If there's anything I can do for you, don't hesitate to contact me." She thought of slipping him a business card but realized he'd have no trouble finding her if he wanted to.

She was considering who to talk to next when Rafe

bore down on her, his gaze and stride filled with single-minded purpose.

"I see you've met my fiancée," Rafe said to Remington as they shook hands.

"Indeed? I hadn't heard. Much happiness to you both." He lifted his glass. Then to Rafe, he asked, "How is your father getting along?"

Hope wondered if Rafe knew everyone here. It was possible since only a fraction of the society's members were present.

He gave a brief overview of his father's situation. Following the murder of his lover, Theodore Sterling had taken a months-long cruise, including a port of call in Morocco, a place he and Lillibet had planned to visit on their honeymoon. He'd scattered her ashes there, and according to him, he'd left his heart there as well. Now he rarely ventured outside his oceanfront condo.

"Grief does strange things to us," Remington agreed, those haunted lines trenching beside his eyes again.

"Good evening, ladies and gentlemen!" A voice, cultured and energetic, blasted from unseen speakers, instantly cutting through the din. "Welcome to our annual holiday party. For those who don't know me..." He paused for the laughs and guffaws that would follow.

Her mouth open, she looked at the emcee and then at Rafe. "Jaxon Mills? Are you kidding me?"

Rafe grinned.

Jaxon owned one of the most well-known and respected digital media marketing companies. He was everywhere, admired by many, despised by some who believed he was a loudmouth. But his success was inarguable. Celeste believed he was somewhat of an oracle when it came to guessing what the next big thing would be. Because he acted on it, he'd come from nothing to amass a small fortune. And he, too, was a Titan?

"Consider yourselves fortunate," he finished. More laughter followed. "I'm Jaxon Mills, your host for the evening. It gives me great pleasure to direct your attention to our chairperson, Judge Gideon Anderson."

The judge, rumored to be a front-runner for the next vacant Supreme Court seat, stood in the semicircle at the top of the stairs. With stunning silver hair, astute blue eyes, and a physique chiseled by competitive running, he was an impressive figure. "A merry Christmas to all!"

Everyone lifted glasses and echoed the sentiment.

"Welcome to our Christmas party and new member induction. It's a delight to have you at the Parthenon. Let the festivities begin."

He made his way down the stairs.

"He needs a wife," Remington said. "It would help his bid for the Supreme Court. Rumor suggests it was a consideration when he was passed over last time. Image is everything."

"Interesting." She'd had a couple of politicians come to her for help, just for that reason. "Maybe I'll chat with Celeste about it."

"I'd like to see him appointed. No one deserves it more."

When the judge reached the lobby, the crowd parted to let him through, and he walked toward the doors leading to the dining room.

"Enjoy yourself," Remington said. "If I decide to consider a relationship again, I'll be in contact."

Rafe had informed her they were assigned to table three, and it didn't take long for them to find their place cards.

She was next to Rafe, and there was an empty chair to her right. Rafe was seated beside a woman who ran an exclusive travel arrangement company. According to her, they didn't just book hotels, homes, cruises. They created experiences. It might include a cruise, but on a ship that would stay in port long enough for guests to spend several days in a Norwegian fjord and a night under a glass dome to see the Northern Lights. The woman indicated an interest in chatting with Rafe about the launch of his upcoming exclusive cruise ships, large enough to contain five-star amenities but small enough to be reserved by organizations and able to access locations that bigger liners couldn't go.

Hope was getting tired of nodding while pretending

she could hear everyone else's conversations when a man walked over to the table to pull back the vacant chair.

Conversation died as electricity arced through the room.

"Kian!" Rafe stood, and the two men shook hands. "It's been a long time"

While he wore power as naturally as the other Titans, she'd never seen anyone like Kian. While other members were dressed in tuxedos, he was in jeans and a leather blazer. His tie was looped in a careless knot. His hair was a little too long, a lot too mussed.

A tattoo streaked up from beneath the collar of his white button-down shirt, stamping bad boy all over him.

She shook her head to stop staring at him.

"Did you ride in?" Rafe asked.

"From Dallas."

"In this cold?"

"I froze my—" He broke off abruptly and looked at Hope with a halfway apologetic tilt of his head. Then he flashed her a sincere, pulse-stopping smile. "I beg your pardon, ma'am."

"Allow me to introduce Hope Malloy, the future Mrs. Sterling."

"Ah. Congratulations are in order. Kian Brannigan." He extended his tattoo-covered hand. "It's a pleasure to meet you."

Recovering her manners, she slid her palm against his

as she looked up, meeting his eyes, and suddenly she saw beyond the obvious good looks and practiced charm to the pain laced in his eyes. He was here, at the party, but at the same time…not.

A waitperson walked toward him, carrying a cut-crystal glass on a silver platter, interrupting their greeting.

Banishing the fanciful thoughts about a man she didn't know, Hope eased her hand from his.

Rafe returned to his seat, and Kian sat in the chair next to her. In a single swallow, he downed his drink, then signaled for another.

"You rode in? Like on a motorcycle?"

"Yeah," he confirmed. "Prefer it to a car."

"Most people would fly that distance."

He was silent for a few seconds. "Most people, perhaps."

His second drink arrived, and this time he stared into for a moment before taking a sip.

Since he'd arrived late, he opted to skip the salad and go straight for a rare steak. "Tell me about Hope Malloy."

"I'm a matchmaker."

He put down his fork. "Are you?"

"Don't worry." She gave him a reassuring grin. "I'm not soliciting clients."

"Thank God. I'd go broke if I hired you to find me a

wife."

"Tell me about Kian Brannigan," she invited a few minutes later, when he'd loosened his tie even more and allowed his shoulders to relax.

"I build custom rides. Motorcycles."

"High-end ones," Rafe supplied, leaning in and placing a hand on her thigh.

Awareness of her man went through her in a wave so powerful she lost the thread of the conversation.

"He also races them," Rafe added.

Kian tipped his glass toward Rafe. "You're welcome to stop by the shop, or the track."

"I'll do that." He nodded. "Might be an interesting option to offer our hotel guests." Keeping his hand on Hope, he turned back to the woman next to him. "What do you think? Could be some sort of package? Staying at a Sterling property and touring Brannigan Custom Bikes, perhaps a day or two of racing school, followed by a day at the track?"

Further conversation was interrupted by the arrival of coffee and dessert. A few minutes later, Jaxon announced that the program would begin in fifteen minutes.

Rafe looked at her with his eyebrows drawn together. She recognized this particular type of smile. He intended to suggest something wicked, way outside her comfort zone. Something she both hated and liked. To the rest of the attendees, the way he leaned toward her would appear to be endearing and intimate. "This would be an excellent time for you to excuse yourself to the ladies' room to masturbate."

Even she hadn't been prepared for his words to be so filthy, at odds with this grand event.

"Since I'm edging you, you will stop before you come." He lifted her hand to his lips. "Please return to me with your juices on your fingers."

Her breath whooshed out.

"Do you understand my instructions?"

"But—"

"Do you understand my instructions?"

"Yes, Sir," she whispered, her traitorous body already responding to his seduction. Life with him would always be interesting. She picked up her handbag, and he stood to pull back her chair.

"You please me," he murmured.

Pretending her life was as ordinary as everyone else's, she made her way to the restroom. Unnerving her, there was a waiting line, and she took her place at the end.

When it was her turn, her cheeks were heated, as if everyone knew what she'd be doing in the stall.

Her hand shook as she hung up her clutch, then lifted her dress to brush a finger across her clit. From all of their play earlier and his constant reminders, her body was already aroused. Her gentle touch made her gasp, and she yanked her hand away.

When she returned to the table, he would no doubt ask how long she'd pleasured herself. He'd see through any half-truth, and she didn't have the courage to admit she'd quit after a couple of seconds. That would be a recipe for him taking her back to the cottage, uncaring whether or not they missed the ceremony. Whatever punishment he doled out would be so much worse than enduring this.

With determination, she pressed her lips together so she didn't cry out as she swirled her first two fingers around her clit. The tiny piece of flesh swelled, but she continued until it throbbed.

In order to avoid an orgasm, she had to stop while she caught her breath.

All around her, conversation buzzed. She was grateful the hiss from the electric hand dryers drowned out her tiny whimpers.

When she was in control again, she slid a finger inside her pussy. The memory of Rafe splitting her apart as he had probed her depths rushed through her. She closed her eyes and tipped her head back, lost in thoughts of being his submissive while she fucked herself.

Within seconds she was panting, so very close to coming. Her fingers were slick with her own juices, and she had to lock her knees to stay upright. She wanted the climax. Needed it. It would take a handful more strokes to put just the right amount of pressure on her clit...

It took all her control to pull away her hand and allow her dress to drop.

She grabbed the door hook until she could suck in a couple of deep steadying breaths.

Hope wasn't sure how her legs supported her, but she squared her shoulders, unhooked her bag, then left the stall.

She busied herself at the sink, rearranging her hair and touching up her makeup, stalling while she struggled for composure. Finally, a minute later, she exited the ladies' room.

Surprising her, Rafe lounged near one of the marble pillars. Rather than take her back to the ballroom, he led her to a private alcove beneath the magnificent staircase. Because people were getting ready for the event, some at the bar, others making final trips to the restrooms, no one noticed them.

"I want every detail," he said, voice roughened with arousal.

"I'm so…" She sighed. *Overwhelmed.*

"You played with your clit?"

"A couple of times…" She licked her lower lip. "I fucked myself with my hand until I couldn't take any more."

With one eyebrow cocked, part curiosity, part frown, he waited.

"I stopped before I came."

"That's my girl. Now give me your fingers."

She trembled anew as he lifted them to his mouth and licked them. In the bedroom, that was erotic. Here, now, it was scandalous and threatened to make her come.

"You didn't wipe yourself when you were done?"

A threat made his voice rough, shooting a tremor through her. "No, Sir."

In the distance, Jaxon boomed a five-minute warning.

"Go wash your hands." Rafe released her.

With a nod, she hurried to obey. She was losing herself in him, but the deeper she went, the more he was there for her.

CHAPTER THREE

Rafe pulled back Hope's chair, waiting while she seated herself. Instead of moving away, he stroked her neck. She shivered, and the same lightning that had clearly chased through her at his touch now went through him.

He loved this woman and was always delighted with her, and tonight, more than ever. In a few minutes, she'd take her rightful place among the Titans, then, soon, as his wife. For a man who'd spent his adulthood avoiding relationships, Rafe was besotted.

At one time, she'd demanded to know if he wanted a spine-tingling attraction to someone who consumed him, a wife he couldn't stop thinking about. He'd said he didn't. And now…lucky bastard that he was, that was exactly what he'd gotten.

After almost losing her, he'd invited her into places in his life that no other person had witnessed. And it had strengthened their commitment. She demanded a lot from him, but she gave so much more in return. He could no longer picture coming home to an empty house.

Even if she wasn't there, the Colonel was. Hope's feline was a bossy and moody Somali cat who, for some reason, liked him. Whenever she thought he wasn't giving her enough attention, she'd pounce on his lap, claws bared, unconcerned about any damage she might cause. Sometimes she slept on top of his head. Regularly, she burrowed beneath the bedcovers to curl up between him and Hope.

His life was fuller than it had ever been, and it promised to get better. Hope had indicated she was willing to entertain with him, and there were strategic business alliances that might further his firm's interests that he was eager to pursue. Having a spouse who was a Titan, with her own connections, and understood the workings of the Society, would no doubt be advantageous. A baby would complete the picture perfectly.

The overhead lights flickered, a silent indication that the ceremony was about to begin. Most people returned to their tables, but Kian had vanished, not that Rafe was surprised. The real surprise was that Kian had attended at all, unless he had reason to be in New Orleans or the South. A new lead he was chasing? A memory he was outrunning?

Around them, conversation faded to vague whispers.

Heavy velvet curtains at the front of the room parted, and Jaxon took to the stage to introduce Rykker King, the chairperson of the membership committee.

Rykker started with warm holiday wishes then began recapping a few events from the year. He read off a list of financial contributions to philanthropic organizations and announced the year's scholarship winners. That led to a video of Zetas doing charity work overseas, even showing a couple of their doctors on a medical mission in Africa.

A few minutes later, clips were shown of member efforts stateside, working on recovery after a devastating hurricane, numerous pet adoption events, and a nationwide drive for foodbank contributions. Their service days were highlighted, where Zetas traded suits and heels for hammers, hardhats, power tools, and paintbrushes. In all, the members had donated over twenty million dollars and contributed thousands of volunteer hours.

The video ended, to thunderous applause. Rafe nodded, an odd warmth in his heart. It wasn't sentimentality because of the holidays or the love he had for Hope. To him, the ability to be of service was the best part of being a Titan, and he was damn gratified by the work they did.

As the lights came up, Rykker went on. "Tonight, we introduce twenty new members and the latest addition to the steering committee. We'll begin by acknowledging those who are in attendance this evening. Please welcome our chairperson, Judge Gideon Anderson."

The man waved as he walked across the stage to take his place at the far left. As Celeste's name was announced, she sashayed onto the stage, her gown shimmering in the light. Next came Senator Susanna Brady from California, in a sequined black dress—the first time Rafe had seen her in anything other than a business suit. Cullen Montgomery, CEO of a data mining firm, followed.

Once the clapping had ended, Rykker spoke again. "As you no doubt have heard, Theodore Sterling has resigned his seat. Over two hundred years ago, in 1865, John Sterling was one of the original five founding Zetas. Since then, a Sterling has always had a seat on the steering committee. We thank Theodore for serving our organization."

There was another pause while members clapped. For years, before the overwhelming responsibilities that Theodore hadn't wanted had worn him down, he'd been a hard worker. He'd made Sterling Worldwide stronger, and he'd shown up for all the Zetas' meetings. Theodore deserved this moment of appreciation, and Rafe was sorry his father wasn't here in person to accept it.

"In keeping with proud tradition," Rykker went on, "we are delighted to have Rafe Sterling as the newest member of the steering committee."

This time, thunderous applause rocked the ballroom.

Hope grabbed his hand and squeezed tight.

Having her beside him meant more to him than the honor of taking his seat as one of the leaders of the Zetas. "Thank you for being here."

"I love you, Rafe."

He leaned in for a quick kiss. At the illicit taste of her, need—stunning in its ferocity—blasted through him. Part of him ached to yield to his caveman-like instincts, toss her over his shoulder, and carry her back to the cottage, witnesses be damned.

Scarlet flooded her cheeks and she dropped his hand. "Go," she urged, as if reading his mind. Not that it was difficult to guess what he was thinking.

He made his way to the stage to shake hands with Rykker. Rafe greeted each of the other committee members before reaching Gideon to accept the official gift, a lapel pin, crafted into the Zetas' symbol.

As Gideon placed it, the weight of responsibility settled on Rafe. Though he'd been filling in for his father at recent meetings of the steering committee, being a full member humbled him.

Even from across the room and with the glare of the bright spotlights, the warmth in Hope's gaze reached him.

Once his part was over, Rafe took his place at the end of the line and waited through the inductees until Hope's name was called and the spotlight found her. Rafe's breath was tight as he watched her thread her way through the tables and toward the stage.

Her gown flowed, the long slit revealing a creamy thigh. He'd been stupid to edge her tonight. He hadn't just denied her. He'd denied himself, as well. He should have fucked her hard and fast. And in future, he might do that...take her while she was dressed in formal wear, maybe bend her over the couch, or, even better, have her lie on the bed with her legs behind his head. He could get off while refusing to let her come. The only thing better than her juices drying on her thighs was the thought of his seed there as well.

He glanced at his watch, calculating how long he had to wait to claim her.

One of the volunteers assisted Hope as she climbed the stairs. Instead of walking straight to the podium, she stopped in front of him. "Congratulations, my darling." Rafe said into her ear so the microphones didn't pick up his voice. "I figure we can have a glass of champagne, mingle, share a dance. An hour?"

"Yes, Sir," she whispered.

Rykker cleared his throat in a good-natured way.

With a flirty smile, Hope continued on. Because Celeste was her sponsor, she was the one to present Hope with the box containing her Zeta Society ring.

She posed for a picture between Rykker and Celeste

before another volunteer assisted her from the stage.

The rest of the presentations dragged on, and Rafe knew he had a lifetime of ceremonies to look forward to. The truth was, he normally didn't mind. But tonight, because Hope had agreed to set a wedding date, he was eager for some personal time with her. He was more than serious about being ready to start a family.

When the event concluded, he was slowed by the well-wishes of attendees, and numerous people had questions about his father. By the time he reached the table, Hope wasn't there.

He found her in the lobby, champagne in hand, talking to a small group of people. He appreciated the way she engaged with others, and that he didn't have to worry about her at social events.

Rafe ordered himself a drink, then sought out Eldon Misken for the coveted autograph. Most people wanted signatures from musicians or actors, but then, there was nothing ordinary about Hope or Skyler.

"Small price to stay at the Parkland."

Rafe grabbed a cocktail napkin. While the Parthenon's name wasn't on it, there was a picture of the Grand House. With luck, Skyler would be so thrilled to receive the signature that she wouldn't ask about the logo.

"Who's it for? Your future wife?"

"Her associate, Skyler. It's a Christmas gift."

Misken covered the entire napkin before handing it

over to Rafe.

"Thank you. Seems a little odd to ask for autographs. The only time I'm asked for a signature is when I'm committing my soul to a financial deal."

Misken clapped Rafe on the shoulder. "Perhaps one day you'll be famous." He picked up his martini and walked off.

Rafe glanced at the napkin.

For Skyler—

Reach for the stars.

At the bottom, Misken had scrawled his name and added a drawing of the rocket that had made his company famous. Rafe wondered if Misken had intended it to be phallic.

To keep the paper from wrinkling, Rafe wrapped it around his wallet and tucked part of it inside to hold it in place, taking care not to create deep creases.

The moment Hope spotted him, she smiled and excused herself from the conversation. When she reached him, she flashed her ring.

"It suits you." He grinned.

She admired it from a dozen angles. "It does, doesn't it?" Then she pointed to his lapel pin. "Ooh-la-la! That's fancy! You're a big shot now."

"As if I wasn't already?"

"Well, now you're an even bigger big shot. I'm so

proud of you, Rafe. Every day. Every way."

Mindless of who might be watching, he kissed her.

"My toes just curled," she said when he pulled back. "How long did you say we had to stay?"

"It seems being a bigger big shot comes with more obligations. Let's talk to a few people, and I would like that dance I promised my future bride."

Music shattered the conversational buzz.

Her mouth dropped open as she obviously recognized the opening notes. When the Zetas hosted events, they hired the best musicians and actors. Every event was memorable.

"That sounds like Crescendo." She named one of the biggest classic rock groups in history.

Rafe lifted a shoulder in a casual shrug. Being a Zeta had some perks, and he enjoyed her discovery.

"Is it?" She shook her head in disbelief. "It can't be. They play stadiums. They received a lifetime achievement award last year."

"You like the group, I take it?"

"Are you kidding me? We won't mention the amount of money I paid for tickets when I saw them in Houston."

"Shall we go in?"

Then the lead singer hit the first words of the number. "That's them!" Hope exclaimed. "It's definitely not a tribute band."

Along with scores of other people, they entered the grand ballroom. Three bars were set up, along with numerous tall tables. There were no chairs, not that anyone would want to sit, anyway. The group, fronted by two sisters for more than two decades, was renowned for their rock—some of it hard—tunes as well as some acoustic ballads that highlighted the older sister's stunning talent. They'd made a name for themselves because of their huge range, some songs starting with haunting lyricism and ending on a crash of heavy metal.

"I can't believe this!" Hope shouted to be heard. "I work out to this song!"

Rafe took great pleasure in Hope's delight. They enjoyed the first half before heading back into the lobby during the intermission. Together, they wound their way through the crowd, congratulating new members, discussing business, renewing friendships. Two men and a woman indicated they might be interested in learning more about Hope's matchmaking services.

"I don't think you're getting a Christmas vacation this year," Rafe warned. "Lots of opportunities to set people up for New Year's Eve."

"We have one mixer scheduled. Maybe we should add another."

"Can't hurt," he agreed. "A lot of companies are closed the week between Christmas and New Year's. That makes it an ideal time. Though I'd rather have you to myself."

"What would you do with me?" With over-the-top innocence, she batted her eyelashes.

"I think you have an idea or two."

She waved a hand in front of her face. "Whatever could you mean, Mr. Sterling?"

He laughed at her pretending-to-be scandalized tone.

Crescendo returned to the stage, this time opening with a slow, romantic ballad that had won a major award for best movie score. "Would you like to dance?" Rafe asked.

"I'd love to."

He'd do anything for her smile.

Once they were on the dance floor, she surrendered into his arms, as if she had always been there.

"What do you think of your first event?"

"I'm a bit overwhelmed, to be honest. I keep wondering if someone is going to pinch me, and I'll wake up to discover everything with you has been a dream." She lifted her hand from his shoulder to admire her Zeta ring once more. "Then there's this."

"There is, indeed."

"And this." She wriggled her ring finger.

"Both pretty solid, I'd say."

"Like you, Mr. Sterling." As the song moved into the chorus, she lowered her head to his shoulder. "If it is a dream, I want to stay in it."

They fit together seamlessly, and he didn't want to let her go. Dancing gave him another way to make love to her. Even though they were one of dozens of other couples, he had a sense they were alone, that nothing existed but the two of them and the music. She stayed where she was until the final notes trailed off.

Then, because the band was playing more songs she adored, they moved to the back of the room to enjoy the show. The performers segued into one of their most popular numbers, and at least half of the members and guests crowded in front of the stage, as if they were at an actual concert.

The band invited the crowd to join in. And on the chorus, the lead singer turned her microphone the opposite way to feature the gathered crowd.

Applause rang out as the final notes filled the air.

Hope turned to him. Because the din of applause rocked the room, she stood on tiptoes and leaned into him. "I'm not sure how much longer I can wait. Would it be okay if we leave now?"

The need to possess her clawed at him in a primal urge. "Nothing I'd like more."

"Remember to come back so we can scan your biometrics now that you're official, Ms. Malloy," Fitzgerald, the head of security, reminded her as they were leaving.

"I'd forgotten."

The Parthenon had a state-of-the-art security system

in place, meant to protect the estate, but the scanners also made it easy for members to get around while they were in attendance. Room keys weren't needed. Doors and gates opened automatically.

Rafe asked Hope to remain inside while he had the valet bring the car around.

Within minutes, he had her back at the cottage. His deliberate click of the lock made her turn in his direction.

He still loved that about her—the way her eyes widened when she realized she was his prey. Rafe crooked a finger. "Please come here, Ms. Malloy. You owe me thanks for the autograph I secured for Skyler."

Her mouth parted. "Are you kidding me? You actually got it?"

"Did you doubt I would move the heavens for you? Here. Now." It would be easy enough to go to her, but at times, he preferred to exert his power.

Her shoes made little strikes on the hardwood floor. He liked the way her gown moved, presenting him a quick glimpse of her legs.

When his beautiful wife-to-be was in front of him, she tipped back her head to meet his gaze.

"Please remove my tie, Hope."

Her fingers trembled as she reached to pull the knot from the black silk. Once she had, she left the ends dangling on his white shirt.

"And my belt."

She fumbled a little, and her hand brushed his cock. It sprang to life. With a quick, indrawn breath, she glanced up again.

"At this point, I've decided not to subject myself to any unnecessary suffering."

"I'm sorry you're miserable." Her smile was teasing, and not at all contrite.

"I won't be for much longer. You, however, will be uncomfortable for some time. Consider it penance for your sass."

With a small wince, she asked, "How about if I apologize?"

"Too late."

Still shaking, Hope managed to release the buckle. After she pulled the leather free of his pants, she curled it into a large circle.

He extended a hand. "I'll take it."

With a deep, bracing swallow, she gave him the belt.

"Thank you. Now go sit in that chair." He pointed to a high-back antique piece near the fireplace.

After she'd taken her seat, he draped the length of leather over the back of the settee. Aware of her gaze tracking his every move, he grabbed his bag of BDSM equipment from the corner and placed the expensive piece of luggage on the coffee table.

She knew he'd brought a number of their toys with

him in the hope they'd visit the Quarter. So far, she'd been hesitant, and he refused to go without her. Even if they never went, the BDSM that they already shared would be more than enough for Rafe. What bothered him was that she hadn't been forthcoming about her reasons for not wanting to attend. When asked, she offered vague half answers or gave mumbled excuses. On occasion, she changed the subject. Now that they were in Louisiana for a couple of days, they'd have time to sort it through. "Any particular implements you'd prefer this evening?"

They'd been together long enough for her to realize that she might not have a choice, that the decision was ultimately his.

"I assume you have something in mind, Sir?" Her voice was soft in a way that told him she'd already started to slip into a different part of her brain.

Over the years, he'd played with numerous subs, but his connection with Hope was unique, perhaps because they shared all parts of their lives. He knew her well, what turned her on, what comforted her. To think he'd spent so long avoiding this kind of commitment astonished him. Then again, maybe he'd been waiting for Hope. "I do."

"Then I want whatever you want."

"My sweet Hope…" He walked to her. That hadn't been part of his original plan, but he had to touch her and show his appreciation for her.

Rafe captured her shoulders and drew her up, then he took her in his arms and lowered his mouth to hers. On her lips, he savored the tang of champagne and the Dominant thrill that accompanied her response. It was headier than any alcohol. In this relationship, his heart had been pried open, revealing tenderness that he hadn't known before. He would protect her from anything, even at the cost of his own life.

When he ended the kiss, her lips were swollen and parted, and pure desire radiated from the depths of her amber eyes. When she was aroused, the color became more golden than hazel. That was why he'd selected a yellow diamond for her engagement ring. Nothing else matched her radiance. "I'd like you naked, except for your choker and engagement ring."

He loved the sight of her nude body. When he remained clothed, she seemed to sink further into her submission to him, and her reactions were magnified. Rafe released her shoulders and took the seat she'd vacated. "Undress for me."

She removed her Zeta ring then wriggled out of the dress and allowed it to drop to the floor.

With her spine erect, her shoulders pulled back, her breasts high and tantalizing, she started to step out of the puddle of chiffon. He raised a hand to stop her. "Stay there while I look at you."

Previously, she'd told him that this kind of request unnerved her. "Spread your legs and part your labia." There was nothing he enjoyed more than sending crashes of sensual adrenaline through her.

For a second, she hesitated.

He lowered his voice and infused it with a harsh whisper that threatened retribution. "Don't make me ask again."

She held her breath and remained in a place.

"We can use clamps if you'd rather not do it your-self."

"No!" She moved a hand between her legs. "I mean, I'll do it, Sir."

"I thought that was what you meant." He struggled to suppress his grin.

Then, with obedience, she pulled her pussy lips back.

"Beautiful." He planned to spend their entire future letting her know how perfect she was for him. "Keeping yourself spread, walk over here. I want to punish your clit."

She flinched. "That sounds painful."

"Most certainly. I intend it to be."

With great pleasure, he watched her internal struggle play out in her eyes. She knew she'd come hard later. *Was it worth it?*

Hope stepped over her dress. He exhaled with pure pleasure as she made her way to him.

"I'm not sure I've seen anything sexier," he said.

Their gazes locked as she stopped in front of him.

"Closer," he ordered, unable to keep the growl of possession out of his voice. She was *his.*

After a slight hesitation, she inched toward him.

"I want to be comfortable while I do this to you."

Her breaths were strangled, despite the fact that he'd yet to touch her.

"Enough hesitating, Hope." She had a safe word to put an end to this, and she had a second word that would allow her to slow down the scene. In all the time they'd been together, she hadn't used either. They'd talked about that more than once. He'd affirmed that it was okay for her to use one. It wouldn't change the fact that he adored her or was impressed by her.

But her response had been the stuff of dreams.

Unquestioningly, she trusted him with her body, and he treasured that. He enjoyed taking her to new heights, but he would always be careful with her, and he wondered when she'd show the same emotional trust by joining him at the Quarter.

Her breathing still shallow, she took another step, so that her pretty pussy was near his hand.

"Yes. Exactly right. How many seconds should I do this for?"

"Please, please don't make me answer that."

"I was thinking ten to start with."

She pressed her lips together.

"Another three for stopping too short. Four more for hesitating when I told you I wanted you closer. And, let's see…five seconds for refusing to respond to my question. Count up the seconds." He moved his hand closer to her flesh. His submissive was already damp, turned on by his language and the threat of her impending punishment.

"Uhm…" She started to pull away.

"I wouldn't do that if I were you," he said in a conversational tone. "You don't want to tempt me to make it longer, do you?"

"No, Sir!" Immediately, she jutted her hips forward so that she was right near his hand.

"Better. I'm still waiting for the count."

"Oh… I can't."

"How many? Or we can call it a round thirty. Half a minute of the most exquisite pain I've ever subjected you to."

"Twenty-two."

"I knew you were better at math than you were letting on."

She moaned.

"Lower your cunt toward me."

Eyes wide with a hazy mix of fear and anticipation, she bent her knees.

"Don't let go of your pussy lips. You're an active participant in this. You will count, and no rushing the numbers. To make it easy, we'll do it this way—one-one thousand, two-one thousand, and so forth. Failure at any part, including you moving away, will mean we need to start again."

"What if I can't do it?" Doubt laced her broken words.

"You can. Just imagine how thrilled I will be with you. And the reward you'll receive later."

She swallowed.

"It would have been over already if we had gotten started right away," he pointed out. "Drag it on as long as you like. We've got all night for your fear to build and your fingers to tire and your pussy lips to get sore. You know, we could add some nipple clamps as a distraction." He owned a pair that she didn't mind, and several that she swore she detested.

"Please squeeze my clit, Sir."

"That's my brave submissive." He dampened his first finger and swirled it around her clit, making the nub swell.

She rocked forward, begging—without words—for an orgasm.

"I revere everything about your body. Playing with it, tormenting it, pleasing it." He paused. "Claiming it."

"Yours," she whispered on an exhalation.

"So charming. Ready?"

She gritted her back teeth and nodded.

"I want to hear it."

"Yes, Rafe. I'm ready."

"Count out loud." That would force her to breathe, which would make it easier for her to endure. He clamped down hard.

She yelped.

"Hope," he encouraged.

"One thousand one…"

"Keep going." He increased the pressure until she wobbled.

"One thousand two…"

When she reached ten, he slipped his free hand around her waist, not just to steady her, but to give reassurance.

"One thousand eleven…"

Her breaths were broken little gasps as her struggle reached a fevered high. "Keep your pussy lips open so we don't need to start over."

At fifteen, he moved his free hand between her legs so that he could slide a couple of fingers inside her to ratchet up her pleasure.

"Oh! Oh…" She swayed as she struggled to remain upright.

"Keep going." He eased deeper into her. When she managed to gasp out fifteen, he leaned forward to kiss her belly.

As she continued to count, he fucked her with his

fingers as he whispered words of encouragement.

"One thousand twenty-one."

"So good."

The moment she said, "One thousand twenty-two," he extracted his fingers and released her clit.

When the blood flow returned, she screamed, and he opened his arms to catch her. "You may let go of your pussy lips."

As he'd expected, she collapsed against him. He scooped her up on to his lap, and she turned into him, snuggling his chest.

He held her and stroked her, loving her until her breathing returned to normal.

"Fuck, Sir. That hurt."

"I imagine you'll be extrasensitive for some time."

"That didn't sound sympathetic." She placed her hand flat on his chest and pushed back a little to look in his eyes. "In fact, you seem rather pleased."

"I am. Every time I caress or fuck you, lash your pussy or even lick it, you're going to squirm more than usual. Just think how rewarding your orgasms are going to be."

"Not that I would know. It's been forever since you got me off." A pouty note hung in her words, which wasn't like her at all.

"Really? Forever?" He grinned at both her white lie and her petulant tone. "In that case, I think you can wait a little longer."

"But…" She scooped hair back from her face. "I can't tell if you're serious or not."

"I am. Very much. But I want you, Hope, and I'm going to have you, right this minute."

CHAPTER FOUR

Hope didn't often miscalculate her future husband. After enduring that torment, she'd expected him to give her a world-shattering orgasm. Normally, he was both generous and indulgent. But right now, she was confused. It was as if she was seeing a different side of him.

Though he'd edged her before, it had never been for this long or this intense.

He nudged her from his lap, and she glanced away, trying not to show her frustration.

Rafe stood to capture her chin. He tilted her head back a little, so she couldn't look away from him. "Have I ever left you unsatisfied?"

When it came to Rafe, she couldn't hide her reactions. "But—"

"Answer my question." His tone reassured but also left her no room to wiggle out of answering.

"No, Sir. You haven't. But you've kept me waiting

when you want to drive me wild." A zillion needs crawled through her, confounding her, demanding satisfaction. Her clit burned from his handling, and her pussy was wet from the way he'd finger-fucked her. She was more than ready for his cock. She wanted it. Needed it.

"So why would tonight be any different?"

"Because I made you mad?"

He frowned. "You didn't. Not at all. I see your struggle, and that's okay. We're broadening the scope of our BDSM play and navigating that may be difficult from time to time. You will never disappoint me." He placed his free hand on her shoulder to emphasize his words. "I love you too much."

"Then—"

"Nice try." He massaged her skin, moving his fingers in small circles. "You'll get your orgasm when I'm ready to give it to you."

She didn't want to relent. "I shouldn't have asked you to edge me earlier this evening."

"Perhaps not." He grinned. "And yet, here we are."

He was so tall and handsome and dominant that he left her breathless.

During their exploration of her sexuality, he'd introduced her to dozens of new toys and experiences. Because of their demanding schedules, they didn't get to play as often as either of them wanted to. But they'd made a commitment to ensure that they never lost track of what was most important in their lives. Each Sunday, they compared calendars to set a date during the week that they would be alone so they could enjoy an extended scene.

On those days, she tried to get home before him so that she could shower and dress in something he'd set out for her before he left for the office. She'd be waiting for him when he arrived, in a place and position he'd texted to her sometime during the afternoon. If she wasn't able to arrive home first, he enjoyed watching her get ready, monitoring her every move.

He released her chin to trace the lines of her choker. "Begging may be rewarded. Asking nicely might also. I prefer to set the pace and decide what I think is best for you, for us."

"Even if I don't like it?"

"Especially then."

"All this talking is delaying my orgasm, isn't it?"

"One of the things I admire best about you is your keen intellect."

She smiled, everything inside of her softening. At times, it was as if he understood her reactions better than she did. He'd said all the right things to ground her and deal with the flash of annoyance.

"Are you ready to continue? Or would you like to step away from BDSM for tonight?"

He might not be disappointed in her if they stopped the scene, but she would be disappointed in herself, and that was something she couldn't live with. She tipped her head back. "I'd like to go on."

"Knowing your orgasm is mine to give, when I wish, *if* I wish?"

As he'd no doubt intended, the *if* tormented her. It was possible he'd deny her until the next day. Or worse. She knew she could always use her safe word, but she wasn't tempted to use it. "Yes, Rafe."

"Very well." He released his grip on her, and her skin was still heated from his touch. "I'm ready to come. One of us deserves to."

One of us? Meaning he was thinking about coming? But after everything, he'd deny her? Her first reaction was pissiness, and she forced herself to bite back a frustrated reply.

"You can finish undressing me."

He didn't request this often, and she almost always liked doing it for him, the same way he enjoyed taking off her clothes.

Rafe extended one wrist after the other toward her, and she obliged by removing his emerald-studded Zeta cufflinks. She placed them on the coffee table before returning to pull his bow tie free. She placed that around his cufflinks. Next, she helped him off with his jacket and hung it from the back of the chair.

She reached around him to unfasten the cummerbund. Every inch of his body was familiar and reassuring. As if knowing how much she needed the connection, he hugged her, tucking her beneath his chin and holding her tight. The tiny, remaining pieces of resistance she'd experienced earlier began to slip away, replaced by love and trust.

"I appreciate this," he said, his breath warm on her. "I appreciate *you.*"

His words and touch were all she needed. After he let her go, she folded his cummerbund and set it down.

This evening he'd worn studs in his shirt, and it took her several seconds to slide them free. She placed each in the circle she'd created with his tie.

As she drew his shirt off, she trailed her fingers over his flat abs, enjoying the smooth strength of his body. She glanced up, thrilled they had a lifetime ahead of them to explore each other. For the first time, she was glad he'd moved up the wedding date.

Hope knelt to untie his shoes, then tucked his socks inside them. When she was done, she looked up at him. The position and her nakedness at his feet reinforced her submission in a way nothing else could.

"Continue." He nodded.

After releasing the button at his waist, she tugged down his zipper. Rafe hadn't worn anything beneath the slacks, and his engorged cock throbbed in front of her face. Need swamped her as she lowered his trousers.

"Why don't I have you do this more often?" he asked, his hand in her hair, making a tight knot.

"Perhaps you should, Sir."

He released his grip to squeeze her nipples.

The punishing pleasure made her moan.

When her mind was reeling, he offered a hand up, and she accepted. Giddy, she gathered his clothes and folded them, placing them near his belt. Once, he'd used it on her, and it been one of the more intimate things they'd shared. The fact that the supple leather was still warm from his body had excited her.

Now it was there, like a serpent, taunting her.

"I want you on the bed, on your back. First, take off your shoes."

She grabbed hold of the back of the settee for balance as she followed his instruction.

"And Hope? While you're still there, grab the belt," he said.

She went still. Had he read her mind, again? No matter what she wanted, he seemed to know.

"I saw your eyes. You can't hide anything from me."

While the leather's bite had been sexy, its sting lingered as a phantom memory. Aware of him watching her, she picked up the belt and carried it to him.

"The bedroom, Hope."

She loved the urgency in his voice. Knowing she

drove him as wild as he drove her sent a thrill rocketing through her.

While they'd been out, the staff had turned down their bedding and left expensive chocolates on the pillows. For safety's sake, she moved the foil-wrapped goodies to the nightstands before pulling the comforter all the way off, so she could lie down on the sheet.

"Scoot to the edge of the mattress," he instructed. "I want your feet to touch the floor, or as close as possible. And spread your thighs as wide as you can."

When she was in position, he stroked the insides of her legs, making her squirm.

"Would you prefer to place your arms beneath you or shall I secure them?"

Which meant he was going to do something she might not enjoy. Her breath caught. "I'll keep them in place."

"Very well." He waited while she moved herself around until her hands were tucked beneath her buttocks.

He continued to move his hands across her, adding a little more pressure with each pass, heating her skin while being careful to avoid her pussy. The fact that he avoided her most private places sharpened her desire.

Rafe dangled the belt near her face until the strap filled her entire vision.

"Oh…" Adrenaline spiked through her. She had no

doubt about his intentions. Hope railed against the instinct to close her legs and protect herself. "I…"

"Your choice," he offered. "Stay by my will or I can fetch restraints."

Without waiting for her answer, he brought down the leather on the inside of her right thigh, above her knee. A burning sensation ripped through her, but it receded right away, unlike some other implements where the pain lingered. She liked it. Before she had a chance to articulate her realization, he struck her again, a bit higher. The moment she'd processed it, he added a third, dangerously close to her pussy.

"Three lovely stripes," he said. "Look." He slid a hand beneath her back to help her sit up.

She studied the lines. Each was beautiful, spaced with precision. "I like them."

"Good." He grinned. "So do I." He lowered her to the mattress again.

Hope knew he wouldn't use his full strength on her, but it still took all her determination to keep her legs wide for him.

He delivered the next three strikes with the same deliberation, igniting a maelstrom of emotion in her. She yearned for his cock, a physical connection, even if he didn't get her off.

Rafe dropped the belt on her tummy, and the buckle was cool on her skin. "I want your legs over my shoulders."

Since she couldn't do so without help, Rafe assisted her into position and tugged her hips toward him, meaning her ass was suspended in the air, and she was dependent on him to help her keep her balance.

"Are you ready for me?"

She didn't need to answer. He inserted a finger to find out for himself. When he found her G-spot, she almost came. "Not yet," he reminded her, removing his finger. The truth was, when he touched her like that, she couldn't fight her climax. He controlled it, and he knew that.

"Now about my orgasm." He took hold of his cock and pressed the head into her.

She sighed, and her whole body relaxed. Hope needed this.

"That's it. Let me take what I want." He nudged deeper and deeper, and he lifted her legs higher, then pressed one of his muscled arms down on her pelvis, keeping her in the position he preferred.

"*My God!*" She gasped when he moved, filling her pussy until his balls were against her ass. *So damn deep!*

"I've wanted you all day." His voice was growly, needy.

Even though they'd had sex last night, she was as consumed as he was.

He slid in and out with slow strokes, driving her

mad. There wasn't enough sensation for her to get off, and with the way he held her, she couldn't change positions. "This is impossible, Rafe."

In response, he put his free hand beneath her hips, further imprisoning her. "It's just right," he countered.

Over and over, he drew out before filling her again.

She wasn't prepared for the way her body shook when he changed tempos, driving in and pulling out with rapid-fire speed. "Rafe!" Hope was going to come if he kept it up.

He touched her clit, and she screamed from the fresh wave of pleasure spiced with a tinge of pain. Before she could recover, he leaned forward, his shoulders pressing the backs of her thighs, giving him even greater access to her body.

He fucked her hard, overwhelming her. If he hadn't been so forceful about restricting her movements, she would have been left shattered.

"I'm going to come in you…"

Until he spoke, she hadn't realized her eyes had been closed. She opened them to focus on him. Possession painted the spikes in his eyes with steel.

"Fill your hot pussy and leave you dripping."

"Yes…"

"Ask me."

"Come in me, Rafe. Mark me as yours."

His answering moan was guttural. He thrust in once

again and stilled. Then he groaned as he made some shorter, more stuttered strokes.

His features contorted. Hope loved knowing she affected him this way. It was a special kind of power, and until she'd been with him, she'd never known it.

After he'd ejaculated, he eased back and smeared some of their juices all over the insides of her thighs, still hot from his belting.

"Your pussy was made for my cock," he said, tracing one of the welts with his damp thumb.

Each touch reminded her that her orgasm had been denied, yet she forced herself not to ask about it.

Rafe allowed his still-formidable dick to slide from her before easing away from her and helping her to lower her legs from his shoulders. "Wrap yourself around me."

She placed her calves on his hip bones while he assisted her on to the bed once again. "Trapping my arms beneath me works as well as bondage," she murmured.

"How are you doing?" He massaged her shoulders.

"Fine," she replied, hoping he wouldn't use her exhaustion as a reason not to continue their scene.

When he tipped his head to one side, she propped herself on her elbows to meet his gaze. "I promise.

"In that case, go into the living room and open the toy bag."

She accepted his help to sit up, curious, but in a nervous sort of way. He'd packed not just for their weekend at the Parthenon but also for a trip to the Quarter…one that he thought she was ready for.

As Hope started to move past him, he snagged her wrist.

"I'm not sure how I managed without you in my life," he admitted.

This time, she kissed him. "I don't even like to think about alternatives."

His smile was quick and devastating. "Then get going." He released her.

She hurried into the living room, and he was right behind her as she opened the bag. On top was a stunning bright purple halter top dress. She scooped it up to look at it more closely. The front took a scandalous plunge while the skirt was full and would stop well below her buttocks, about midthigh. "It's gorgeous."

"For the Quarter," he said. "I'm not pressuring you. I brought it in case you want to go. If not, it stays in the bag."

"You have to know I love the color." In fact, she liked everything about the dress, including the cut and the silken material. She wanted it.

"It will look good with your hair."

No doubt it would also flatter her figure. On the rare occasion she'd allowed herself to contemplate what it might be like to go with him to a BDSM club, she'd imagined he'd want her garbed in the same sort of outfit she'd scrolled past online, a harness, perhaps formfitting leather, or that popular shiny PVC material. This was not even close to scandalous. In fact, she had a few summer dresses that were every bit as revealing.

"It will suit you." He watched her carry it to the mirror.

It shouldn't surprise her that he'd made such an excellent selection.

Hope wouldn't be ashamed to wear this in public. His purchase had been a smart calculation. Because the dress was wonderful, he was making it easy for her to say yes.

"Set it aside for now," he encouraged before she was ready to let it go.

After a second glance in the mirror, she returned to him and placed the dress on the table, near where she'd left his accessories.

"What would you like to play with tonight?" he asked, as if the question about the club had not arisen.

He'd brought a great number of their toys. Her favorite small flogger as well as the stingier rubber one. He'd included a tawse, a devil's tail, and a paddle that bore the word *Princess*. At the bottom was a wand type of massager as well as one that covered her clit. She prayed he didn't want to use either of those.

"You choose one, and I'll choose one," he suggested.

Her insides lurched. She supposed it was better than

him selecting both, but his words made her nervous, nevertheless. "The rubber flogger."

"Excellent. I can work your whole body that way."

Her mouth dried as she waited for his decision. He reached into the bag and pulled out the dreaded small massager.

"This should be fun."

Since he wouldn't allow her to come until he was ready, he obviously intended to make her whimper as she lost control of her body.

"I want you to stand for this. Lace your fingers above your head." Rafe returned to the bag for soft cuffs to wrap around her wrists.

"I don't suppose it will do me any good to point out that you already picked a toy."

"None at all," he agreed, grabbing a second set of cuffs. He attached each to her elbows and used a strap to hold them together. "How's that?"

"Fine. Thank you." She supposed she could lower her arms with some contortions, but since it would displease Rafe, she would fight to hold the position. At home, they had hooks in the ceilings of a couple of rooms to prevent her escape.

He tested the vibrator to make sure all the settings worked. As he approached, she skittered back a couple of steps. "Believe me when I tell you that you don't want to avoid me."

"Sorry, Sir." She was contrite, but damn, she didn't want that terrible thing gyrating on her still-tormented clit.

He inserted three fingers in her pussy to hold her in place while he placed the toy and made sure the suction cup grabbed plenty of her flesh. He turned it on the lowest setting while he double-checked that it wouldn't fall off.

Even that small amount of sensation was enough to make her squeeze her buttocks in a vain attempt to get away. "Oh, Rafe."

"No coming until I say."

The edging clawed at her, becoming a physical ache in her stomach. Realizing he was waiting for an answer, she gave a tight nod.

"I'm going to warm you up before the flogging begins."

"Yes, Sir."

He notched the vibrator up, just a bit. The annoying thing clamped down on her flesh. Then he left her there, bound and helpless.

An orgasm teased her, and she jerked. "Sir!"

"Already?" He tsked.

She wished he'd get on with it, so that she could escape the device.

He returned with the rubber flogger and he drew it across her body, down it, in sensual lines that left a trail of goose bumps. "I love the way your nipples get so big."

Rafe worked his way around her with a little more force. It wasn't yet enough to grab her complete attention or allow her to surrender.

Instead of thinking about the toy shuddering against her in relentless waves, she focused on the sensations of the dozens of strands of thin, flexible rubber.

Rafe circled her again, catching her nipples and the insides of her legs.

"You ready?"

Too overwhelmed to answer, she simply nodded.

He stroked down her jawline before stepping away. Flogger in hand, he stood tall and fierce, intimidating.

"You're going to have to fight yourself to give me what I want."

"You want me to wait," she whispered.

He turned up the vibrator again. With a yelp, she danced around, trying to escape, but it was relentless. He didn't attempt to make her stay still. Instead he used the flogger on her, between her legs, shifting the toy.

With artful motions, he flogged her front, catching her breasts and nipples, making her scoot away from him—not from pain but because the sting intensified the ache in her pussy.

She gulped for air as he blazed her ass. Nothing existed outside the awful sucking sensation, the sting of his whip, and the drug of his reassuring words.

Rafe! She wasn't sure whether she'd begged aloud or whether the reverberation played in her head.

He went on, sizzling her thighs, her knees, then lower to the fleshy parts of her calves.

She was dizzy from the constant fall of the flogger, but he wasn't done with her. He worked her sides, then her ass again.

Hope existed in a sensual fog, breathing deep, trying to please her Dom.

At some point, she realized he was no longer flogging her. And the lack of the distraction intensified the vibrator.

"You're spectacular," he said, turning the thing off.

She was drained of energy, and her body went limp.

"Take some deep breaths." He made quick work of releasing her cuffs and rubbing her arms before removing the vibrator.

As he scooped her up and returned with her to the bedroom, she murmured her thanks over and over.

"You're so very welcome." He placed her on the bed, then crawled between her legs. "Hold your labia apart."

She wasn't sure she could.

"Hope!" He barked the word, garnering her instant compliance, even though her hand shook.

Rafe wet a finger and teased her clit, manipulating it.

She clenched her butt cheeks. His touch was beautiful and painful, leaving her teetering on the precipice that he'd forbidden.

"I'll let you know when."

Hope closed her eyes and began counting down from one thousand, trying to distract her mind by giving it something difficult to concentrate on. Rafe's gentle teases were enough to crash through her defenses. She made tiny sounds of frustration, trying to hold on to her composure.

When she couldn't endure another moment, and her slow word was crowding her mind, he moved his hand away. She exhaled and released her pussy lips.

"No." Though his word was soft, steel underlaid it.

With a small whimper, she once again held herself open for him. She arched in shock when he placed his mouth over her pussy and began to lick and suck. "Oh, Rafe!" Normally she got lost in his oral skills, but tonight it was nothing short of pure misery.

"Do you want to come, little subbie?"

"I might die if I don't."

He chuckled, but the sound was more diabolical than a humorous one.

"Please, Sir." She lifted her head to look at him. "I don't know how much longer I can do this."

"You may release your grip."

Grateful, she collapsed against the pillow. Then she discovered he wasn't done with her.

He continued to tongue her, then slide his fingers in

and out of her pussy.

An eternity later, he moved his mouth from her and slid his heavy cock inside her. She exhaled a ragged breath as he filled her, and it shocked her that he was ready for her again so soon.

"Kiss me," he said, squeezing her breasts, twisting her nipples, then capturing her mouth.

Her essence was on his lips, adding to her own passion. He kissed as intently as he fucked. He demanded her gaze. When she met it, she swam in the heady combination of lust and love radiating from his eyes.

"Anytime you're ready," he said, the words such a relief she almost sobbed.

Hope bit her lower lip as she surrendered to his powerful strokes. From his flogging as well as his belt, there wasn't a part of her body that didn't tingle.

Letting herself relax, Hope spread her legs wider, no longer fighting her own responses.

"That's it," he approved.

They moved together, and pure bliss unfurled. "I'm…"

In response, he thrust harder and held her wrists tighter. He knew her so well. She ground the pads of her feet into the mattress, so she could lift her hips a little higher to change the angle of his thrusts.

She screamed, spiraling as the orgasm engulfed her.

He murmured something she couldn't make out. She

wasn't aware of him letting go of her wrists, but he was cradling her face when reality returned.

"How are you doing?"

"I could sleep for a week," she admitted. "And I might."

"You've earned it." He began to move with slow, gentle thrusts. This time, her desperation was gone, replaced by fluid languidness that added to her lethargy.

Rafe pressed himself up onto his hands, and she enjoyed his strokes. The way he brushed her clit was pleasant, making her realize she wasn't as sore as she'd thought. He knew how to lead her to the brink and keep her there. He had an uncanny instinct about her capabilities. Rafe had explained that he studied her responses, facial expressions, muscle tension, movements, her sounds. Thinking she couldn't endure one more moment, she'd been tempted to shout out her safe word, but he'd changed his approach, making it unnecessary. After this evening, her trust in him was deeper than ever.

Without urgency, he came in her. Then he kissed her, expressing his appreciation for her before withdrawing to turn onto his side. He pulled her against him and drew her into the cocoon of his arms. She closed her eyes, drinking in the satiation.

"You're an amazing partner. You were magnificent at the event tonight, more than I knew I wanted."

She wriggled her buttocks back, and he groaned.

Maybe she should edge him. The ridiculousness of the idea made her smile. *As if he'd ever allow that.*

"Be careful of what you start," he warned. "Unless you're ready for more?"

"You mean you could do that again?" She turned to face him. "After we've already done it twice?"

His cock surged against her. "Want to find out?"

"No, no." Her response was instantaneous. "Tomorrow's good."

"That's what I thought." He reached behind her to slap her rear once, and that reignited the nerve endings inflamed from the earlier flogging. "Let's get in the shower so we can get to bed."

He was damn good at aftercare. In the enormous shower, he washed her, using copious amounts of lather. He rinsed her pussy, and his touch was perfunctory rather than sensual. After all he'd subjected her to, however, she was somewhat turned on.

When they exited into the steamy bathroom, he dried her and examined her body for any bruising. Satisfied, he carried her back to the bed.

"I'll take care of the toys."

She nodded and snuggled beneath the covers, but she couldn't get comfortable without him. All his sounds seemed amplified, the crinkling of the package that held an alcohol swab, then the hum from the toy.

A tiny part of her couldn't help but think about what

implements he might want to take, if they went to the club. *If...*

He returned a couple of minutes later, carrying her designer gown.

"I can't believe I forgot about it."

"If you had been thinking about it, I would have been doing a bad job as your Dom."

As he hung it in the closet, she couldn't help but think about the purple dress that he'd packed for her. She pictured herself in it, and she wondered what it would be like to accompany him. "What would you wear?" she asked.

Gloriously naked, he turned to her.

"To the Quarter," Hope clarified.

"Black trousers. White shirt."

"Like a pirate?"

"If you like." He grinned. "No eyepatch, though. Sorry if that disappoints you."

Hope gave an exaggerated sigh. "I suppose I can live with it."

"So you're thinking about it?"

"I don't know if I can get past my nerves," she admitted.

He sat on the edge of the bed and faced her. "Are you ready to talk? To be honest?"

She grabbed the covers and pulled them higher for emotional support. "I..."

"We both know how important good communication is."

Hope sighed. He knew almost everything about her, but her own doubts were so big, it was hard to know where to begin.

Rafe stayed where he was, allowing her a little distance between them to sort through her thoughts.

"There are women there that you've played with."

A scowl trenched between his eyebrows as he absorbed what she'd said. Then, after a few moments of silence, he admitted, "I'm sorry, Hope. I don't understand."

"You don't…?"

"I'm trying. We're engaged. I can't wait to marry you and knock you up."

"That's not it." She clutched the sheet even tighter.

"Confide in me."

Before she could lose her nerve, she said, "I won't measure up."

"Against what?" He frowned, as if perplexed.

How could such an astute man be so clueless? "Rafe, damn it. They're submissives. They know what they're doing, how to act. They've pleased you before, and I'm…" A knot of emotion formed in her throat, and she swallowed, trying to dislodge it before it spilled out in tears of humiliation.

"You're what?"

With a deep, pained gasp in her words, she confessed, "Flawed." New. Uncertain.

Shaking his head, he dragged away the sheet and gathered her against him.

"You're not hearing me!" She beat on his chest, and she blinked, losing the battle to keep her fears locked away.

He captured her wrists, not hard, but preventing her from moving. "You're not hearing *me,*" he countered. "It's you I love. There's nothing to measure up to. No *one* to measure up to."

Refusing to meet his eyes, she lowered her head.

"You're the sub I want, Hope. With others, it was about me giving them what they asked for. With us, it's about both of us getting our needs met. Scening at a club is one thing, but I have you twenty-four hours a day. We have a relationship. We laugh, discuss business, sleep together, breathe together. We're planning our future and talking about starting a family. No other woman could ever measure up to you." He pulled back on her hair. "Tell me you hear me."

"But they…"

"Go on, please," he prompted when she trailed off.

"I'm sure they're all confident. They know what they're doing. How to act. The protocols… All of it."

"They're women, Hope." He was scowling, as if still perplexed. "All gorgeous. Like you."

She sniffled. "Was that supposed to help?"

"Did it?" There was a hopeful note in his voice.

"No." Hope frowned up at him.

"Not everyone is experienced in the scene, and you will find the members to be gracious and inviting."

She wasn't convinced.

"It occurs to me I should tell you there is no nudity at the Quarter unless we have a private room."

"And would we?"

"If you wanted to. But I'd suggest we walk around for a while, get familiar with the place. We can visit, with no expectations, if you wish. In a way, it's not all that different from our evenings at Vieille Rivière."

Before her first trip to the members-only restaurant on the banks of the Mississippi River, nerves had almost paralyzed her. But as the evening progressed, she'd grown more comfortable. Things that had shocked her when she walked in had become normal by her second visit.

"Shall I tell you more?"

She wanted to go because it mattered to Rafe, yet she needed to get past her hesitations.

Without waiting for a response, he continued, "In addition to your dress, you'd wear a thong."

"Did you bring me any underwear?" She hadn't packed any.

"Of course."

He thought of everything.

"If your breasts are exposed, you'd need to wear pasties or tape to cover your nipples."

"Are you serious?"

"Of course."

"I've seen more scandalous attire at Mardi Gras. And on a spring break vacation." In fact, some dresses she'd seen in public were sheer enough to show an outline of a nipple.

"There you have it."

"I suppose those are in your bag too."

"Along with a couple of different pairs of stockings and a garter belt, if you would like to wear them."

Although she almost always had bare legs, from time to time she enjoyed the sensuousness of fine lingerie. Since the South was experiencing an unusual cold snap, stockings might be welcome.

Again, he didn't push for an answer, and she appreciated him for it. Instead, he moved them both, so they were lying beneath the covers. "Thank you for telling me."

"You think I'm ridiculous."

"No. I don't," he promised. "And I want you to be able to talk to me about anything."

Though he wrapped himself around her and draped a possessive arm on her hipbone, she was enthralled with visions of what the club might be like and wondering if she had the confidence to submit to Rafe in public.

CHAPTER FIVE

A s if she didn't want to ever let go, Hope clenched her hand around his. That suited Rafe fine. More often, she was turning to him, strengthening their relationship each time. He squeezed her reassuringly. "We don't have to stay if you're uncomfortable," he promised. "Ready?"

She nodded.

He extracted his hand to ring the bell located next to the unmarked green wood door. Then he glanced toward the security camera attached to the building.

When the lock snicked open, he turned the handle. "Ladies first."

After a brief hesitation, she stepped through the entrance.

In New Orleans's French Quarter, it wasn't unusual to walk past a number of doors without noticing them. Some led to clubs, shops that didn't advertise in the usual ways, and upstairs apartments. The club owner also operated a restaurant downstairs as well as a to-go bar serving world-famous hurricanes with lethal amounts of rum, which allowed them to keep the space above it for the kinkier crowd.

In front of him, Hope gripped the rail as she climbed to the second story on her high-as-sin heels. When they reached the top, she moved aside so he could precede her into the lobby. "Evening, Aviana," he greeted the tall, willowy woman.

She came from behind the podium to give him a hug and to kiss his cheeks. "It's been far too long, Rafe."

"It's a pleasure, as always." Tonight, her waist-length hair was bright pink, and she wore a black sarong that skimmed the floor in the back but was cut high in the front, barely keeping her covered. He placed a reassuring hand on Hope's spine. "Aviana is a Mistress and the owner of the club. Aviana, my pleasure to introduce my future wife, Hope Malloy."

With a radiant smile, Aviana took both of Hope's hands. "So you're the one."

"I'm sorry?" Hope asked.

"He raved about you when he made the reservation. You must be a very special woman. I'm delighted to have you at the Quarter."

A nervous exhalation rippled through Hope.

"I have some paperwork for you to fill out," Aviana continued. She led them to a table against the far wall. In recognition of the season, a Christmas tree had been plonked on the table. It was decorated with naughty ornaments, whips, handcuffs, etchings of couples and moresomes engaged in illicit acts. While she extended a pen toward Hope, he placed his bag on the floor.

Aviana outlined a few things Hope needed to know. "The club's safe word is *red*. If you use it, one of our dungeon monitors will step in. They'll be wearing black vests with a gold fleur-de-lis on them. As your sponsor, Rafe will be responsible for your behavior. We don't allow nudity unless it's in a private room. We do have a bar that's open until three a.m., but we do not permit you to imbibe if you're playing. If you order a drink, we mark your hand with an X, and if you're caught scening, you can lose your membership. Except for bottled water, no beverages are allowed outside the bar area. Also, no interfering with anyone else's scene. Please watch from a respectful distance. If you have questions as to whether something is okay, please ask a monitor or Rafe."

Hope nodded.

"Will you be using a scene name?"

"It's your choice," Rafe told Hope when she turned her head toward him for guidance. "A few people I know use a middle name or a combination of their initials. Others a nickname or something that strikes their fancy. I'm comfortable with you doing whatever you wish."

Aviana took over by explaining, "The privacy clause

prevents members and guests from acknowledging each other outside of the club, unless both parties agree."

"What do you do?" Hope asked him.

"I go by Rafe."

"Then I'm fine using my name." She scanned the agreement before affixing a shaky signature to the bottom.

Rafe placed his hand on her nape to massage away the tension. She exhaled, soft and slow, and it gratified him to know she responded so completely to his touch.

Addressing Rafe, Aviana said, "Please sign here to acknowledge your sponsorship of Hope."

He did so.

"Hope, after three visits, you'll be eligible to apply for your own membership. That would permit you to attend without Rafe."

"That won't be necessary." He struggled to keep a snarl from his voice.

Aviana grinned. "So that's how it is."

"It is."

"The coat check is open." She scooped up the paperwork. "Enjoy your evening."

"Milady." He inclined his head.

Aviana moved off to greet an arriving foursome.

Rafe drew Hope toward the cloakroom located to the left of the podium. "May I take your jacket?"

She loosened the belt, then hesitated before removing

her peacoat and also turning over her purse.

Rafe secured a claim ticket for her items. He considered keeping his bag in case she wanted to play, but then thought better of it. If they had no way to scene, she might relax more. Hearing her ask him to collect their toys would be a joy.

"You look beautiful," he said to Hope when the clerk departed. Before they left the cottage, he'd wrapped her neck with the multistranded necklace that served as her collar. With every breath she took, the tiny diamonds sparkled, much like her eyes.

She'd opted for fishnet stockings and a garter belt with the dress. When she slipped it on earlier, he was taken aback. He'd known it would be stunning, but it was more than that. It was perfect. The front snuggled her breasts, showcasing their delicious plumpness. The waist fit snugly enough to highlight the flare of her hips. He was torn between keeping her in the dress and giving in to the urge to rip it off and fuck her until she couldn't remember anything except his name. "Let's have a walk around to get your bearings."

"So far, I'm doing okay."

A frosted-glass door with a fleur-de-lis etched into it separated the reception area from the dungeon.

Before crossing the threshold, Hope paused. Loud music thumped through the air, reverberating through him. He waited for her to process it. Then, much sooner than he anticipated, she entered of the dim room of her own accord.

Off to the left was something that appeared to be a bit of an obstacle course. It had a wall that wasn't too high, a long tunnel contraption, a web of ropes a couple of feet off the ground with a crash pad beneath, a balance beam, and a tank of water that appeared to be about three feet deep. It hadn't been here the last time he visited, and he imagined it would be used for competitions among submissives. *That could be interesting to watch.*

At the far end of the open space, a massive wooden throne sat on a raised dais. "For Mistress Aviana," he said against her ear.

"That's impressive."

"It was a gift from an admiring sub. You can't see the detail from here, but her likeness is carved into the top, and the rounded arm ends were custom-made from a plaster cast of her grip." The upholstery was velvet. And there were hooks in the wood of the dais where she could chain her submissive du jour.

Rows of Saint Andrew's crosses were scattered throughout the area, along with numerous spanking benches. Nearby, a sub was being subject to a single lash, and the crack of the leather echoed. Elsewhere, a Dom yanked away his partner's pants, leaving the man wearing nothing but a skimpy gold lamé thong.

Since Hope was all-but gawking, Rafe suggested, "Let me show you around." He kept his hand on her as they moved to the right, where the bar was located.

The area was enclosed with thick glass, making it much quieter than the dungeon. The polished bar had been reclaimed from an 1800s pirate lair—if legend was to be believed.

Aviana had selected Louisiana-proud as her theme. A stuffed tiger represented LSU. A neon sign from the local brewery hung from the ceiling, and shelves were lined with Saints' helmets, alligators, trumpets, saxophones, carnival masks. Photos of local landmarks adorned the walls, and there was a cardboard cutout of Riptide, Tulane University's mascot. Mardi Gras beads were wrapped around hurricane glasses, and a server was dressed as if she were on a paddlewheel boat, with a brocade vest and a garter encircling her upper arm.

Rafe leaned in toward Hope. "They have your favorite champagne."

She turned to him. "You asked them to?"

"I sent it over."

"You think of everything."

"We can have a drink at the end of the evening. Or, after you've had a look around, if you decide you would rather not play, we can enjoy the bar."

She looked at an empty table then back at the dungeon. After wetting her lower lip, she admitted, "I think I want to see more."

Unable to hide his pleasure, Rafe smiled. "So brave."

They walked through the main area and stopped to watch a rigging demonstration.

"My God, that's gorgeous," she said when the woman was suspended, and the rigger twirled her around.

"Not my particular expertise," he admitted. "Though I am willing to learn. Or if you want to try with Xander, I'm willing to let you."

Eyes wide, she faced him. "Are you serious?"

"I'd want to be there, of course. And perhaps take pictures. But yes. He's willing to instruct or do private rigging."

"One day I might be interested."

That was such a leap from where she had been that he was speechless.

While Xander released his model, Rafe suggested they continue the tour.

"What are all the couches for?"

"Aftercare. Cuddle time."

"You mean that happens in clubs also?"

"Of course. And if we play, I will meet all your needs, not just physical ones."

"I didn't know."

How could she? "I should have done a better job of explaining what the club is like." If he had, maybe she would have had an easier time discussing her fears. He could have even suggested that they visit during off hours.

He guided her through a door that led to a more secluded part of the club. "The club is shaped somewhat like a U," he explained. "This part wraps around the main area. It affords more intimacy. And it's quieter." All the better to hear her whimpers.

A set of stairs against a concrete wall led to a second floor.

"What's up there?" she asked.

"Private rooms, but there's an observation balcony that might interest you. It provides an overview of the entire public area of the club. Would you like to see?" Her eyes were wide, but she didn't shy away as he thought she might.

"I would," she replied.

In keeping with old-world New Orleans, the railing was wrought iron, with fleur-de-lis artistically linking the bars. The balcony had beads draped around the railing. Rafe guided Hope toward the front to overlook the main dungeon as well as the more out-of-the-way area behind the wall. "That's known as *Rue Sensuelle*. Sensual Avenue. Longtime members often refer to it as Kinky Avenue."

"I see why."

There were a number of authentic-appearing settings, separated by partitions. There was a schoolroom, complete with chalkboard, desks, books, a globe, a map on the wall, and a selection of canes nearby. Next to it was a principal's office, then a churchlike scene with a pew and a kneeling bench. Continuing down the line, there was a makeshift jail cell, a boss's office, an examination table, followed by a pair of stocks set on a platform. Then came the Victorian living quarters, including a brass bed and a stand to hold a basin and water pitcher. His favorite was at the end, a tall rather unremarkable leather chair with various straps attached.

A couple entered the schoolroom.

Turning toward Hope, Rafe asked, "Would you like to watch?"

"Uhm… Yes. I think I would." Surprise lingered in her words. "Do you mind?"

"Not at all." In fact, he wanted to enjoy her reactions.

After the couple had exchanged a few words, and the Dom had given his sub what appeared to be a reassuring pat on her rear, he pulled out a couple of implements from his toy bag and laid them on the table before returning to her. In a sharp tone that carried toward them, the man said, "You will learn your lesson about cheating on your test, young lady."

"Oh, Sir!" she wailed. "I'm so sorry. I swear it won't ever happen again!" Full of contrition, she fixed her gaze on her saddle shoes. But then she gave a quick peek upward again.

"I shall see to it."

The man pressed his hand on the sub's back, forcing her to bend over. She was dressed in over-the-knee socks and a plaid skirt, and she obediently grabbed her ankles. Next, the Dom wedged her panties between her buttocks, then pulled the material tight, showing off the swell of her mound.

Hope gripped his forearm.

"Are you shocked?" he asked against her ear.

"Interested," she replied. Her breathing quickened as the Dom picked up a ruler.

He placed it against the woman's ample bottom. The sub lifted her head, but he pushed it down again, her hair spilling around her.

"I can't imagine looking like that," Hope confessed.

"What do you mean?"

"So... She's so into it. So... I don't know. Sexy."

"My darling sub." Hands on her shoulders, he turned her to him. "You're every bit as glorious. And when you're in the throes of a scene, you are wildly magnificent."

She frowned, eyebrows furrowed in skepticism.

"There is no one more gorgeous than you. I'm proud to be with you. You're the sexiest woman here, Hope."

The woman's yelp grabbed their attention and they turned back to watch the scene. Hope dug her fingers into him.

The Dom gave the poor woman at least two dozen strokes, turning her ass a gorgeous shade of pink. And when he helped her up, her face was streaked with tears.

"She's beautiful."

"She is," he agreed. "Are you beginning to understand what you do to me?" After checking to be certain no one was observing them, he lifted Hope's dress and slid a finger between her labia. She was slick. "Watching turns you on."

She nodded and flushed.

"Don't be embarrassed. I was hoping for this." He extracted his hand before smoothing her dress.

Her knees wobbled a little, and he steadied her, cherishing her reactions.

Next, the Dom took his schoolgirl to the desk and had her drape herself over it while he selected a cane. "Are you sure you want to see this? It's going to be more extreme."

"I…" She took a breath. "Yes."

The submissive was given eight harsh strokes, each leaving a searing stripe.

Hope gasped when the Dom traced the lines with a Wartenberg wheel. Then he left the woman there, her punishment on display for anyone who walked by or observed from the balcony.

"What do you think?"

"I'm wondering what it might be like to be her."

"Are you?" When she didn't answer, Rafe didn't push. He wanted her to ask for the scene.

A moment later, they were interrupted by a voice he recognized.

"Excuse me?"

With a smile, and a reassuring hand on Hope, he turned to greet the submissive he'd played with for years. "Sara!"

"I'm sorry to interrupt," she said. "But I wanted to say hello, if you'll forgive me?"

"Hope, this is the woman I believe you called. Sara, I'd like to introduce my future bride, as soon as she'll have me."

Hope's eyes widened at the sight of the beautiful woman. She wore a gauzy two-piece outfit that left her midriff bare. The pants were sheer and flowy while the top was tightfitting. Both accented her feminine curves.

"If you're uncomfortable, I'll excuse myself. I apologize for bothering you." Sara's smile was genuine, as was her sensitivity.

"No. No. I'm sorry." Hope shook her head. "I hadn't expected to run into you, though it makes sense."

In the early stages of their relationship, Rafe had provided Sara's name as a woman who would vouch for him as a Dom. Hope had spoken to her and another woman before agreeing to submit to him.

"You're one of the reasons I took this chance."

"Then I'm glad!" Sara gave Hope a quick hug. "Enjoy your evening. Welcome back, Sir. I'm happy you found your one."

Sara left them, her bare feet silent on the floor.

"I should have thought to warn you," he said.

"She's...graceful."

"She is."

Hope continued to watch scenes in the dungeon. "There really are all kinds of different people here."

He curled a hand around the railing, studying her rather than the crowd. "We kinksters are a varied lot." Young as well as old, and bodies of all types. All were welcome and appreciated for their uniqueness. Perhaps because of the location, the Quarter attracted an enormous variety of ethnicities, education levels, genders, and sexual as well as kinky preferences.

"Sara wasn't what I expected."

"My mother and sister filled out my application for your matchmaking services, not me," he reminded her. "They never asked what I was looking for in a wife." He only needed a few things. Intelligence, warmth, genuineness. And mostly, that she liked having her ass reddened.

"I discover new depths of you every day." She angled her body for a better look at him. "So, hypothetically..."

"Hypothetically?"

"If we were to play here tonight, what would you

want to do?"

"We'd use the room on the end."

After a quick glance, she knitted her eyebrows together. "The one with the chair?"

"Yes."

"What could we do with that?"

"A number of things. I have all our toys and a new slapper." He'd used one on her before, and she'd enjoyed it. This one was different, however. The strike area had three different layers, all different lengths. If he used the opposite side, he'd produce a single strike. If he used the front, his stroke would land in three different spots at the same time. His grip and swing allowed him to adjust the intensity. He was anxious to try it out on her derriere. "I'd start with the flogger and move on from there. Hypothetically." And with the way she'd be strapped to the chair, she'd give herself orgasms like she'd never experienced before.

Her eyes were clear, and her gaze was steady. "I'm ready."

"You're…" His heart tripped, and his cock nudged against the inside of his slacks. "It's important to me that you ask."

"Please, Rafe?" Her voice was steady, sure, a fantasy breathed into life. "I'd like to scene with you here tonight."

The fucking pleasure was all his.

CHAPTER SIX

Rafe had retrieved his bag, and now he placed it on the table in the area where they would be playing. Since he'd first mentioned the Quarter, Hope had exaggerated what it might be like. She'd pictured all the subs as gorgeous females, when in fact a good number of them were male. She'd imagined all men were Doms, yet there were plenty of Dommes, also. Attendees were all shapes, sizes, ages, and a few were garbed as pets, and even some mythical creatures, making it impossible to determine what sex they were. It was liberating. Meeting Sara had toppled the last of Hope's inhibitions.

Rafe hadn't asked her to play out in the open. Instead he'd selected a room that most people wouldn't wander past. It was possible they'd be observed from the balcony, but as she knew, there was so much going on in every corner of the club, and everyone in attendance was involved in their own life.

He pulled out some sanitizing wipes and cleaned all

the vinyl surfaces of the chair. Then he said, "I'm going to put pasties on your nipples."

It wasn't a question. It was a statement from her Dom. The power of it made her shift her weight from foot to foot.

She watched him, his motions sure and confident. The sight of him in the tailored dark trousers and contrasting white long-sleeved shirt made her stare. The pasties he removed from his bag were black silk with hot-pink bows on the front. He affixed double-sided tape to the inside of each cup, near the edge. "Come here, please."

She stood in front of him as he tugged the material of her dress away from her body, so he could attach the coverings. He pressed each against her skin for several seconds to be certain they wouldn't fall off. She shimmied her upper body, trying to get accustomed to the strange weight.

"Unfasten the dress."

She reached behind her to loosen the tie and let the halter top fall away.

"I like the way they look." Rafe's eyes blazed with the first flashes of desire. "Enough to consider having you wear them on occasion. But then, nipple clamps wouldn't work."

Which might be a blessing, though she'd gotten to the point she liked to wear the alligator clips he'd purchased for her. The clovers, she had a love-hate relationship with.

"I'd like you to remove your dress."

She wasn't prepared for that request, and she took a moment to consider it. And then she realized, they were in a scene. His statement wasn't a request. And unless she opted to use a safe word—which she didn't have any reason to—she needed to obey her Dom. "Yes, Sir," she whispered, wishing her voice hadn't broken between the two words.

A trace of self-consciousness lingered, and Hope couldn't help but glance around to see if anyone was watching. No one was. She cast a glance toward the balcony. A foursome stood there, but they were engaged in conversation with one another. One of the couples continued toward the second floor while the other descended the staircase.

"I'm waiting."

The earlier patience in his voice had been replaced by his stern Dom tone, galvanizing her into action. She pulled the dress over her head, and he held out a hand to accept it.

In one of the other Kinky Avenue spaces, a woman wailed, promising to confess as long as she was spared the punishment tawse.

"Straddle the seat, facing backward." Rafe's voice shattered through her thoughts, grounding her. He became her world.

Seizing a newfound sense of empowerment, she strode to the chair.

"And I want your pussy almost on the edge."

The chair was uncomfortably wide and tall.

"That's it. Cant your upper body forward and hold on to the top."

"Oh my God," she said after she'd she followed his orders. The change in position meant her buttocks stuck up a little, and her thong was in contact with the cool vinyl.

He stood in front of her to fasten bonds to her wrists. He tugged her forward, and her feet no longer touched the floor. She was trapped by him. Her heartbeat increased, part from excitement, part from fear of the unknown.

"I've been picturing this moment."

Her mouth was too dry to answer.

He returned to the table, and she watched as he rolled his sleeves up to expose his forearms.

She tried to shift but the leather bondage made it almost impossible.

As if aware of her every motion, he glanced over at her. "Please keep your position."

He has no idea how difficult this is. Hope inhaled as she did as he requested. But watching him reignited her nerves.

Rafe selected the flogger he'd mentioned, one she hadn't seen before. Then she realized the slapper was different as well.

"I want you to enjoy this," he said, hooking the small flogger to his belt loop. He crossed the room again until he stood in front of her.

Her spine was arched in an unnatural way and her inner thighs burned. She was eager to get on with it. Impatience was her curse. But she realized he had become her entire focus. She wasn't looking to see who might be watching.

"You may come as often as you like."

"How?" She frowned.

"By rocking your pussy."

Blood fled from her body. He wanted her to hump the chair? It wasn't possible. She shook her head.

"Your choice." He moved behind her to rub her shoulders and arms. "If you don't want to come, that's fine."

He pinched one of her buttocks and she jerked in response, her pussy brushing against the vinyl. "Oh!" Because her clit was still tender from the night before, this lightest of touches was enough to ripple a shock through her.

She turned her head as much as she could, in time to see him unhook the rubber-thronged flogger. He trailed it over each shoulder, and she shrugged from the

SIERRA CARTWRIGHT

whispered touch.

He began his flogging with a slow figure-eight dance down her skin. The falls stung more than the leather one he'd used on her before, but she liked it. His deft touch was light, meant to tease.

She moaned and dropped her head forward. That caused her to shift again, creating more downward force on the vinyl. She struggled to put her feet down so she could readjust, but she was trapped.

"I should have parted your labia before we started." He continued, bending his knees a little so that he had better access to the strike zone on her ass.

The dozens of strands were everywhere, zapping her skin, heating her. Breath whooshed out, and she allowed the chairback to support even more of her weight.

Rafe increased the speed and force. She whimpered from the sting.

"That sound—your suffering—thrills me," he murmured against her ear.

The first time they met, he'd shocked her with similar words. At the time, she hadn't known he practiced BDSM, and his eyes had sparked with delight each time he ruffled her vanilla feathers. She learned he lived for the noises she made when she was beneath his lash. The more she succumbed, the greater his pleasure.

The little time they'd spent watching others had liberated Hope. The woman in the schoolroom had cried out and pleaded, and there had been no doubt she'd surrendered to the scene, committed to the moment. That gave Hope the courage to cast aside her own inhibitions. Tonight was about her and Rafe, their mutual pleasure, the building of their intimacy, and nothing else.

He pressed himself against her, his body weight further straining her thigh muscles. "Your tears would make this more wonderful."

At one time the inherent threat would have terrified her. Now it turned her on. It meant he intended to push her, demanding honesty, and he was granting permission for her to give all her responses over to him. "Yes, Sir."

"That's what you want, isn't it?" He tucked her hair behind her ear, and she tried to turn her face to look at him. "Isn't it?" he repeated. "For me to make you cry as I cover your ass with my domination and watching you grind out your orgasm like my dirty pet?" He sank his teeth into the side of her neck, forcing her to scream and writhe. "Oh, yes," he said. "I don't often give you permission to come as much as you want. If I were you, I'd seize the opportunity."

He changed positions to grab her ass cheeks and pull back her hips, spreading her legs even farther.

Her tiny whimpers became moans. Her body was on fire, and her pussy was swollen.

"Is the chair slick and hot from your juices?"

She wasn't sure how it was possible, but he inserted a hand beneath her.

"Very wet," he said, triumph ringing in his deep voice. "I think you might enjoy me beating you in public. Anyone at all seeing your reddened butt. Watching the way you respond to me."

"It's you," she admitted. "For you." The truth, the emotion behind her words bubbled up in her, and tears collected in her eyes. Not from pain or humiliation, but from unfettered love. She'd wanted to give this to him, and in doing so, she was receiving so damn much. His adoration and a deeper intimacy. She'd had no idea that this experience would intensify her feelings for her future husband.

"I'm not finished with you."

"I don't want you to be."

He kissed the spot where he'd bitten her moments before. "I'm going to grab the slapper. Less than twenty seconds."

The moment he moved, she missed his touch and wanted him back. Goose bumps dotted her skin as the air-conditioning cooled her.

"Move your body," he said.

Lethargy claimed her, and she wanted to relax in her bondage.

"It wasn't a suggestion."

She closed her eyes and began to slide against the

chair pad.

"Rise up onto your tiptoes and lean forward even more, please. I want access to your pussy so I can spank it."

Dread made her freeze.

"Obey my commands, sub."

Pulse hammering, Hope struggled to change positions. She succeeded in moving a couple of inches.

"So pretty," he said. "So exposed. If you try to hide from me, I will tie you in place." Rafe crossed the room to stand in front of her. His jaw was set in the firm line of resolve. "And to further express my displeasure, I'll give you more than one stroke."

She swallowed the knot of trepidation that threatened to choke her. "I understand, Rafe."

With his fingers brushing the side of her neck, he moved behind her. It amazed her how much stronger she was when he touched her.

He trailed his knuckles down her spine and continued on to examine her rear. "A few faint dots," he told her. "Still, a pretty shade of pink. You'll take the slapper well."

At home, she preferred floggers. Her second favorite implement was a slapper. It was loud and impressive, yet it lacked a painful bite. This one, however, with three distinct layers in graduated lengths, appeared more threatening.

"No need to count. I'll let you know when you're done. Lose yourself. Ride out your orgasms while you turn yourself over to me."

Could she do as he demanded? Block out everything else so that there was nothing in her universe except Rafe's domination?

He fisted his hand into her hair and pulled back her head a little. His eyes were spiked with emotional intensity. "I love you."

She wasn't sure she'd ever been more obsessively in love with him.

He began with slow beats, each at a different place on her buttocks, with no seeming pattern. Almost always, he was somewhat predictable, one on each cheek, or ten on one, then another ten on the other. Other times, he'd place one on top of the other, but always it made sense. This didn't. Five and three. One and then another below it. Not knowing what to expect made it impossible to freeze up, and the gentleness of it lulled her. She relaxed into her bondage, and the tension eased from her body.

Hope closed her eyes. He covered her butt cheeks, but she registered a single impact point at a time. Somewhere in the recesses of her mind she realized that meant he was using the opposite end of the toy.

As he continued, her skin heated. Then when he increased the tempo, she couldn't remain impassive. Her body tried to escape the pain and she rocked her body, bringing her pussy into full contact with the vinyl.

With the slapper, he continued to drive her. Her body warmed, and her toes curled under. "I…"

"Yes," he urged.

She came, screaming out, as if they were alone in the world.

"That's my Hope."

Rather than relent, he turned over the slapper and used it harder. The triple impact points were like needles, and before she could process the searing sensation, he moved on to another place.

She thrashed, unsure whether she was asking for more or trying to get away.

"On your toes," he reminded her. "Open yourself to me."

Scared witless, she nonetheless complied.

He smacked her pussy with all three lines and an orgasm immediately tore through her. She wailed.

"You're so fucking hot."

His words came from another place, not inside her, so very, very far away, but they calmed and inspired. She smiled, sinking her forehead against the chairback, past pain, filled with the rush of endorphins. Hope wanted more, wanted it to go on forever. She was alive and that liberated her.

He continued, and another wave hit her, more engulfing than the previous one because the slapper had lit up her pussy.

She'd surrendered to Rafe and his sensual demands, and she was drunk on it, on him.

Hope rode the crest of another three—*four?*—orgasms. She was limp and surrendered. She slipped away into a fractured space of color, purple and pink, and shards of glass that reflected light, spiraling through her mind.

"You humble me."

His voice was close, too close, and she lifted a hand to swat it away. She liked where she was.

On some level, she recognized that her wrist was free, and she blinked in confusion.

"Welcome back." Rafe wore a satisfied grin.

Pride, maybe?

"I…"

"Subspace is my guess," he said.

"I thought that was mytho—" Her tongue was thick, and she couldn't complete the thought. "Mythologo—"

"Mythological."

"Yeah." She didn't try the word again. "That."

Rafe rubbed her wrists, then ran his hands over her buttocks, soothing away the hurt she was starting to notice. "Take your time."

As if she had any other choice. Lethargy claimed her entire body. He took a towel from his bag and daubed her skin before she cooled too much.

"How are you feeling?"

"I'm not sure yet." As she lowered her arms, Hope glanced up to see him considering her. "Connected. Does that sound strange?"

"Not at all." He shook his head.

"I didn't know."

"Neither did I," Rafe admitted, a ragged scratch in his voice making him sound hoarse.

Hope's heart somersaulted. That he was clearly experiencing the same thing thrilled her.

Slowly, she released the grip she didn't realize she had on the top of the chair. Her hands dropped to her lap.

"When you're ready, I'll help you up," he informed her. "Your legs may have fallen asleep."

She accepted his hand and scooted back. Pinpricks shot through her feet and calves. "Ugh."

He assisted her off the chair, then turned her around. The vinyl was warm and slick from the numerous orgasms he'd driven her to. "Relax there for a moment," he encouraged.

Since she wasn't motivated to do anything else, she watched him pull a small gray blanket from his bag. He wrapped it around her.

Her powerful lover—Dom—scooped her up and carried her from their room, past a few of the other rooms in Kinky Avenue. At the end of the hallway, he lowered her onto a leather couch. "I need to clean things up," he said. "Will you be okay for a few minutes?"

She slid her fingers over her collar. That and his ring were all the comfort items she needed. "I'll be fine." Hope curved against a pillow and snuggled beneath the blanket, enjoying the alternate reality that she existed in.

The sharp click of stilettos grabbed her attention. Aviana strode across the floor, a dungeon monitor at her side. The man was a bearded blond, with piercing blue eyes. He stood well over six-foot-six and was as broad as a massive oak. The only thing preventing him from being a Viking was the lack of a shield and battle-ax. They paused, and Aviana asked, "How are you enjoying the Quarter?"

Hope tried to lift her head and discovered that holding it straight required considerable effort. "More than I imagined."

"It's a lot to take in," she agreed.

"I'm sorry I didn't agree to come before now," Hope admitted.

"Perhaps you wouldn't have been ready."

That was probably true.

"We hope to see you again."

Hope had no doubt they'd return. "Yes, Ma'am. Mistress?"

She smiled. "Milady is fine." Together, Aviana and

the DM continued on, pausing to watch the scenes that were in progress. Hope thought she heard Aviana speaking with Rafe, but since they were so far away, it might have been her imagination.

Aviana and the DM retraced their steps. This time, they continued past without speaking.

A man headed down the hallway, his hands clamped on the bare biceps of two women who were dressed in skimpy maids' outfits. "Please, Sir," one pleaded with an exaggerated accent that made Hope grin. "I promise to do all my work in future!"

"Oh, I'll see to that, wench," he said, dragging the reluctant women toward the Victorian setting. "You'll be too sore to sit down when I'm finished with you."

The second woman squealed, but if Hope wasn't mistaken, it was more from delight than fear.

"Both of you, over the bed!"

Hope's attention was ensnared by Rafe—her lover—walking toward her, her dress in his right hand, his bag in his left. After placing the bag on the floor, he extracted a bottle of water from it, then sat next to her. "Any ill effects?"

"Other than wanting to sleep for a week?"

"You've earned it." He uncapped the bottle and lifted it to her lips.

Though she didn't want any, she took a sip, knowing he would insist on it.

When she was finished, he resealed the bottle. He tucked it away before easing her on to his lap. Hope turned into him, resting the side of her face against his heart. The steadiness of its thump grounded her. Yelps and giggles as well as the sounds of straps being wielded floated around them. She stayed where she was until her pulse returned to normal and her limbs no longer seemed laden with extra weight.

"We can have breakfast in bed tomorrow and then soak in the hot tub. How about we spend the day playing tourist in New Orleans?" he suggested. "Perhaps take in some live jazz?

"Yes!" They'd been to the Parthenon a few times, but they hadn't taken the time to enjoy the nearby city. Work inevitably called, and they both had millions of responsibilities. But the upcoming holidays offered a welcome chance to take a breath.

"Maybe a casual lunch? Dinner?"

"Beignets? Café au lait?"

"Of course."

"Pralines?"

Though she didn't check, she knew the heat of his gaze was on her. "Are you certain you're not already pregnant?"

"I'll have you know, Mr. Sterling, that I can eat sweets and gumbo and jambalaya with the best of them, cravings or no cravings."

"You should be fun when you are expecting."

Again, something leaped inside her. No doubt, he'd be a great dad.

"I'd like to do a little Christmas shopping."

"You?" Using her palm, she pressed away so she could look at him. "Did you just say you want to go shopping?"

"For Jeanine."

His assistant. Of course. Since she had the best gift ever for Skyler, Hope needed something for Tony, her fashion-forward associate. Perhaps a fluorescent tie with jazz instruments on it? Prestige's new assistant also needed a present. Prim and proper, with her pencil skirts, sensible pumps, ever-present glasses and a bun, Miriam ran the office with an efficiency no one realized they'd been lacking.

"Are you ready to go?"

With reluctance, she nodded. Hope hated to move, but she was ready to take a bath, preferably with Rafe, and then go to sleep. Unless he wanted sex, which of course he would. It stunned her to realize how much she wanted that too. She would have thought that she was too sore, but she realized she always wanted his possession.

He scooted her off his lap before standing. "Do you dare go back to the Parthenon dressed as you are?"

She gasped. "In pasties and a thong?"

"You have a coat downstairs."

Could she do that? Walk through the club without her dress? Knowing she might regret it if she didn't try, she nodded. "Of course, Sir."

A slow grin sauntered across his face, and that was all the reward she needed. Rafe packed her dress, the water, and the blanket into the bag, then picked it up. "Please walk in front of me. I want to look at your ass."

Her heartbeat that had returned to normal soared once again as she stood. Hope squared her chin, hoping that she'd become confident if she pretended she was.

"After you."

She walked down the hallway toward the stairs. Her thong was wedged tight between her buttocks, and she refused to stop to adjust it. The hot-pink bows on her pasties glowed in the dimness. As with the scene, no one paid any attention to her or her state of undress. Each minute she was here was easier than the last.

She walked down the stairs with more confidence than she'd walked up them, despite the fact that she was almost naked.

In the reception area, he claimed her coat.

"You've made me a very happy man," he said, helping her into the garment.

During the drive home, she turned on the seat warmer and thought of nothing as she stared out the window.

Once they were in the cottage, he drew her a bath, then removed her pasties before allowing her to take off her underwear and sink into the massive oversize tub. As she'd hoped, he joined her, soaping her and holding her until all tension drained from her body.

"I'd like to visit again," she said.

"My sub's wish is always my command. New Year's Day, perhaps?"

From their condominium, it was a six- or seven-hour drive, depending on whether they stopped at her favorite restaurant in Breaux Bridge on the edge of the Atchafalaya Basin. And if the corporate jet was available, the trip was much faster.

"I'd like that."

"Anything specific you might like to try out?"

"I've been thinking about a plaid skirt."

His cock thickened and nudged against her.

"I take it you're picturing me in knee-high socks, Sir?"

He groaned. "Fuck, Hope."

"Yes, Sir." She grinned. "Let's."

They hurried out of the tub, leaving behind puddles of water and dropping a towel to mop it up as best as possible. He gave her left flank a sharp slap to send her scurrying toward the bed. There, he placed her on top of him. He toyed with her body as she rode him. Because her nipples had been covered for most of their time at the club, she appreciated the attention he gave them.

After he had ensured her pleasure, he came, then held her tight. As she started to fall asleep, he made promises of what he intended to do to her body the next day, starting with an over-the-knee spanking with a ruler in preparation for their upcoming schoolroom scene. "I'm not sure whether to be terrified or excited."

"Both," he told her. "You know, there is a club in Houston, as well. We can go there anytime. So, Hope? If I were you? I'd lean toward terrified."

She shivered, and the sensation was delicious.

CHAPTER SEVEN

"M erry Christmas, Ms. Malloy."

Hope groaned and pulled the pillow over her head. She was still tired from their trip to New Orleans. They'd walked so much two days before that her blisters had blisters. And her ass still hurt from the introduction to his wooden ruler.

Her future husband was an imaginative Dom, but his biggest failing was being a chipper morning person.

He plucked off the pillow, and she scowled. "You'd better have coffee."

"Do I look like a man with a death wish?"

She cracked open one eye. He stood there, naked, with a hard-on and with a cup of coffee in hand. She wasn't sure whether it was the gift or the sight of his toned and rigid body, but she opened both of her eyes.

He set down the cup while he fluffed two pillows behind her. Finally, *finally*, he handed her the magic elixir that would wake her up.

"Thank you." She took a sip before she trusted herself to speak again. "What time is it?" On the weekends, he considered six sleeping in.

"Ten."

"Ten?" she yelped, glancing around for a clock. She hadn't slept that late in years.

"You've got time," he said. "We're not expected at Celeste's until one."

They'd spent Christmas Eve with his mother and his sister, and Hope had enjoyed herself so much that she hadn't been anxious to leave.

"But I did want some private time with you before we leave."

"I'm not sure how much more of your *private time* I can endure, Mr. Sterling."

"We could ride our mountain bikes."

She scooted as far away from him as possible. "Not on your life. Have you seen my ass? Look!" She put the coffee on the nightstand and rolled over onto her tummy. She pulled up the T-shirt she'd borrowed from him to sleep in. "Look!"

He smoothed his hands over her buttocks. "Sorry, darling. There are no bruises."

"What?"

"None. Want me to take a picture with your cell phone so you can see?"

She angled her head to get a better view, but without

a mirror, it was hopeless.

"Your skin is alabaster. Primed for a Christmas flogging."

"Aren't spankings for birthdays?"

"And holidays from now on."

Just then, her terror of a cat tore into the room with a loud cry, jumped onto the bed, then took another leap onto the middle of Hope's buttocks, claws extended.

"Someone else has missed you," he said. "Come here, Samantha." With charming tenderness, he scooped up the feline.

Everyone else in the world called the cat by her nickname, the Colonel, earned for her dictatorial and dismissive ways. Hope flipped over to stare at the two of them. Even though he was cradling the animal, the fur on her spine lifted and she let out another yowling scream. Rafe placed her down, and she raced out of the room and down the hall. It sounded as if she had skidded into the guest room.

"What the hell has gotten into her?"

He lifted one shoulder in a guilty, pathetic shrug. "It could be the catnip."

"Catnip? You gave her catnip? We have rules about that, Rafe." Stunned, she stared at him. "What were you thinking?"

"It was her Christmas present."

He got my naughty cat a gift? What had she done to

deserve this man? But did it have to be something that would make the animal act even worse? Shaking her head, Hope grabbed her coffee. It could be a long morning. "I'm glad we're going out."

Another crash rang out, and he winced. "Why don't you relax and enjoy your coffee?"

"You're in charge of the Colonel."

"That's fine. I'm practicing my nurturing skills for the twins."

"No twins!" She let her head fall back on the pillow. "And no matter how many children, you will be leaving the gift giving to me."

"Spoilsport." He kissed her forehead, then closed the door on his way out of the room. Even though she was sealed off, the thunder of tiny feet meant the cat was still racing through the condo, and Rafe belted out a Christmas tune, charmingly off-key.

She wrapped her hands around the cup and stared into the depths. Was this morning's madness a glimpse at their future? Crazy mornings and inspections of her ass? She grinned. Good Lord, she hoped so.

Humming along with his tune, she climbed from the bed and then attempted to tame her wild, mussed hair before searching out a refill on her coffee.

In the living room, the tree was lit, and there was a massive carpeted structure with perches, a woven rope lattice, a scratching post, and tunnels. "What is this?" she asked Rafe.

He turned from the window. "The jungle gym you brought with you needed to be replaced."

There had been nothing wrong with the other one, and she shook her head, and that was before noticing that catnip was scattered everywhere.

With a sigh, Hope put down her cup.

Wide-eyed, the Colonel dashed in. Ignoring her Christmas gift, the cat raced up the tree trunk, sending glass ornaments smashing to the floor. With frantic meows, she clawed to the top branch.

"Samantha, no!" Hope shouted, hurrying forward.

The star topper wobbled back and forth. Even while Hope was reaching up, it also crashed down and shattered into dozens of shards. How the tree stayed erect when the Colonel launched off it, Hope had no idea.

In his admirable, calm way, Rafe studied the damage and the feline who stood on her new exercise piece, hackles still raised. "Maybe I shouldn't have sprinkled the whole package of catnip on that scratching post?"

"The whole package?" She laughed. "Might not have been one of your more brilliant ideas."

"I'll get the broom and dustpan," he said.

It took less than five minutes to right the living room again, and once they were done, the Colonel continued to zig and zag through the condo.

"She'll wear herself out," Rafe said. Then he followed

the feline with his gaze. "Right?"

She hoped so. "Not sure if that will happen before she exhausts us."

He poured her a second cup of coffee, and then he joined her on the couch. There was a box beneath the Christmas tree that hadn't been there when she went to bed last night.

"Do you mind fetching it?"

"Is it for me?"

"So impatient." He grinned. "Yes."

Rafe took her coffee and moved it to a glass table while she retrieved the box. "Open it," he encouraged when she rejoined him.

Heart racing, she ripped off the dark-red paper.

Her breath sucked from her, leaving her limp at the sight of the diamond necklace.

When they went shopping after the Zeta Society initiation, she'd seen the diamond-encrusted choker in a window display of one of the city's most exclusive jewelers. At the time, he'd suggested the piece might make a good collar, something she'd love wearing every day. Not only would the piece look classy with business attire, it would be just as stunning with an evening gown. They'd gone inside, and when the owner named the price, she'd refused to try it on.

Now, she couldn't take her eyes off it. Along with dozens of tiny diamonds, the teardrop-shaped pendant radiated beauty, refracting the Christmas morning sun. It took her breath away. Her heart thundered. She had to force words past the constriction in her chest. "Does this mean what I think it does?"

"I'd like to ask you to wear my collar full-time."

"Oh... I..." She was as giddy as the night he'd proposed, so breathless she couldn't respond.

"Merry Christmas, Hope." His voice held a waver that told her just how important this moment was to him. "Say you accept?"

"Yes," she whispered.

"Let's go back to the bedroom. I want you to watch in the mirror."

Cradling the box, she stood.

"I'll follow," he said. When they entered the bedroom, he positioned her in front of a mirror before taking the box from her. "I want you naked."

Unlike previous times in her life, she didn't hesitate in baring herself to him.

"Gorgeous, in every way."

She met his eyes. There was no one she'd rather be with.

"Please lift your hair."

While she did, he lifted the necklace from its beautiful box.

Standing behind her, he kept her gaze captive in the mirror. "This is no longer a necklace. It's so much more, a symbol of your submission to me. It represents a transition in our relationship, a greater commitment on our journey together, a heightened level of our understanding and trust. It's also a promise from me that I will care for you as no other. I will protect you, and I will honor you. Do you accept my collar, Hope?"

A marriage ceremony couldn't carry any more weight than this moment. "I do, Sir."

The weight of it settled around her neck, and the pendant nestled into the hollow of her throat. She stared at it and him.

"You've made me a very happy man, once again."

"Oh, Rafe…Sir…"

He turned her toward him, and she raised her mouth for his kiss. He took her offering, coaxing at first, then deeper, with demand. She surrendered herself, lost herself.

Then, in the distance, something else crashed.

Rafe reluctantly ended the kiss with a sigh. "Definitely getting us ready for kids."

She grinned.

"We'll deal with that later," he promised, and he left her long enough to close the door. "First, I want to mark you as my sub. Your first duty is to fetch the short flogger and the paddle. We're going to Christmas dinner with the word *princess* blazed on your ass and perhaps the backs of your thighs. If I do a good job, you won't be able to sit down at all."

Nerves, adrenaline, excitement crashed through her as her mind slipped into another place, where nothing existed except for Rafe and the world they created.

"Did you hear me?" He raised one of his eyebrows in his threatening, intimidating way that had more power than ever to arouse her.

"I did, Sir." She hurried to the closet. By the time she returned, carrying the toys he'd requested in her outstretched palms, he'd attached long straps to a hook in the ceiling. He secured her wrists with cuffs, then clipped them to the strap above her head. She guessed this position meant he intended to start with a sensual flogging. It wouldn't be about anything other than her bliss and his pleasure.

"This morning, as part of your Christmas gift, you may climax as often as you are able."

He gave her one more kiss before pinching one of her nipples and toying with her pussy. He teased her, brought her to the brink, then stopped what he was doing...curse him.

He cut a diabolical grin in her direction. "But because it's Christmas for both of us, I won't make it easy for you."

"I accept your challenge, Mr. Sterling."

He flicked his wrist and caught her with a sexy bite of leather. "In that case, it will be a very merry Christmas for both of us, my sweet, sweet Hope."

I hope you loved Rafe and Hope's journey toward greater trust and commitment. Rafe first met his beautiful matchmaker when he was ambushed by her (and his mother and sister) in his office. She was hired to find him a bride. And he decides only she will do.

Billionaire's Matchmaker

His mother closed the door behind her with a decisive *click*, sealing him in with the enemy. Hope was a beautiful, seductive temptress, but the enemy, nonetheless.

"You're a matchmaker," he said.

"It's an honorable profession."

"Is it? Much like operating an escort service. I hire you. I will end up paying to fuck a woman, one who's interchangeable with any number of other *candidates.*"

"That's as insulting as it is crass." She set her chin and didn't sever the connection of their gazes, meeting the heat of his anger with cool, aloof professionalism.

He wanted to shake it from her, strip her bare, discover what lay beneath the surface to leave nothing but aching, pulsing honesty between them.

Either not noticing the tension or ignoring it, she continued. "Throughout history, families arranged marriages all the time. In parts of the world, it still goes on. Today, there's a bigger need for my services than ever before. I have clients all over the world, from all sorts of backgrounds and of all ages. Often, men in your position don't have time to meet women in the traditional way. You're far too busy, important, insulated."

"Spare me the sales pitch." Rafe took his seat and left her standing. It was undoubtedly rude, but justified. "So that's what's in here?" He flicked a glance at the pile of folders on his desk. "A money-hungry bride-to-be—I beg your pardon, *candidate*—who understands what she's getting herself into?"

"These women all deserve your respect."

"And an expensive engagement ring?" He glanced at the top folder as if it were rabid. "How did you choose these particular women?"

"In normal circumstances, I meet with a gentleman so I can get a sense about him. Then he fills in a questionnaire. It's rather detailed. Fourteen pages of likes, dislikes, things that worked in previous relationships. Things that didn't."

"Go on."

"Expectations around traditions are important as are roles in the relationship. To some, religion is important. I find out if he wants children. If so, how many? Will he want them raised in a particular religion? Where does he plan to live? In the US or abroad? Will the children attend private school? Boarding school? Will a nanny be hired? A housekeeper? After I've reviewed that, I have a second meeting with him for further clarification."

"And they need you for this?"

"Most of the men I work with don't have the opportunity to meet women they might be serious about marrying. They've often focused their attention on their careers or education. Some of them are famous, but they don't want to settle down with a woman they've met on the road or someone who's been part of their fan club."

"And where do you find the women who are anxious to throw themselves at the feet of these rich men?"

"I belong to a number of organizations, and I'm active in Houston's art and business communities. It may surprise you, but I'm often invited to high-society events. I've seen you at a few."

Rafe regarded her again. "We haven't met." He would have remembered. Her eyes, her voice, the sweet curve of her hips, the way her legs went on forever in those shoes. Yeah. He would have remembered.

"No. I spend most of my time talking with women. Part of my value is that I've met all the candidates, interviewed them, watched them interact at social events." She nudged a folder toward him. "Try me."

"Have a seat." Rafe wondered at his sudden offer of hospitality. He didn't need Hope and her lilac-and-silk scent in his office while he looked through the files.

She sat opposite him, her movements delicate. Her skirt rode up her bare thighs, just a bit. He imagined skimming his fingers across her smooth skin while she gasped, then yanking down her panties, curving his fingers into the hot flesh of her ass cheeks.

Christ. He'd spent all Saturday working on next quarter's business plan. In the previous day's bike race against some of his friends, he'd pushed too fast, too hard, on a grueling part of the course and crashed. He'd had a shot of Crown before going to bed, but skipped taking anything else for the pain. He'd slept like hell, and he'd spent too long working out cramps in the shower to even think about masturbating.

Now, he wished he had taken the edge off.

Of course being this close to an attractive female after an intense drought would give him an erection. *Shit.* He couldn't force himself to believe his own fucking lie. Every day, he was surrounded by beautiful women. He wanted Hope. With her ass upturned, listening to her frantic breaths as she waited for his belt…waited for his touch. It was more than the sound of her voice or the innocent-yet-provocative shoes, it was carnal desire. Lust. The last time he was gripped by its power, he'd been in college and far more helpless than he was now.

He imprisoned his thoughts and focused on the task in front of him.

Picking up the first file, he flipped it open.

The top page had a name, a picture, and the vital statistics of a beautiful twenty-four-year-old blonde. She was a UT Austin graduate, a pageant winner who flashed a tiara-worthy smile and worked as a fundraiser for underprivileged schools.

Of course his mother would approve. And yet… He felt nothing—less than nothing. He was uninspired and disinterested. The hard-on he'd been sporting vanished. He glanced up at Hope Malloy.

"She doesn't appeal to you?"

"Not in the least."

"Perhaps you'll have better luck with another choice?"

He didn't.

After perusing the second picture, he glanced back at Hope.

"Nothing?"

"No."

"It's possible the attraction would develop after you meet someone. Her choice of conversation, the way she moves or looks at you." She shifted. "Pheromones."

Those, he was starting to believe in. Keeping his mind on the folders, he said, "I see. My mother hopes I will select a bride, whether I want to fuck her or not?"

Hot pink scorched Hope's cheekbones before she recovered. "So, you would rather have a spine-tingling attraction to someone who consumes you? A wife you can't stop thinking about?"

"No." He flipped the folder closed without reading any of the pages. He refused to be out of control over a woman ever again. But if he was expected to marry and produce an heir or two, he should at least want to go to bed with her.

"Can you tell me what it was about the first two candidates that didn't suit your needs? It will help me refine the search."

"Ms. Malloy..." He struggled to leash his raging impatience. "Show some fucking mercy, will you? Until ten minutes ago, I didn't know I needed a *candidate*."

She edged the third folder toward him.

With great reluctance but with a sudden urge to get through this, he thumbed it open. Another blonde. Another perfect smile. Another impeccable pedigree.

"Since I didn't fill in your forms, I assume it was my mother who decided what college degrees and background were important?"

"Your sister rounded it out as far as activities you enjoy."

"Yet I don't see any of them who like to ride a mountain bike."

"Not a huge demand in this part of Texas."

For the second time, he resisted the impulse to hurl the files in the trash. Instead, he opened his top drawer and swept the offensive lot inside, then slammed it shut.

Hope uncrossed her legs and leaned toward him. Then, evidently thinking better of it, she sat back and recrossed them.

He swore her skin whispered like the promise of sin.

"Perhaps you should consider the options at a more convenient time," she suggested.

"I'll see you receive full payment." He stood.

"I've already received it."

His mother had written this woman a check for a hundred grand? "Thank you for your efforts."

"Mr. Sterling—"

He walked past her to the door and opened it.

She sighed but stood. After gathering her purse—a small pink thing shaped like a cat, complete with ears and whiskers—she joined him. Instead of leaving, as he'd ordered, she stood in front of him, chin tipped at a defiant angle.

Hope projected competence, but the heels and fanciful handbag gave her a feminine air. A sane man would think of her as a vendor or business associate, so he could slot her into the *off-limits* part of his conscience. She wasn't a potential date or wife. Or submissive.

He wanted her.

She isn't mine.

Fuck his conscience.

The super long, intrigue-filled story, Billionaire's Matchmaker is brimming with sexual tension. Warning, you may stay up too late reading! Read more HERE.

sierracartwright.com/titans/billionaires-matchmaker

Have you met the super-sexy agents from Hawkeye Security? Read more about Hawkeye operatives Wolf Stone and Nate Davidson, along with Kayla Fagan in Come to Me, a super sexy, ménage, spiced with intrigue.

If you like two sexy, dominant alpha males, a steamy touch of BDSM, some great suspense, and a heart-wrenching second chance at love, this is the story for you! It's a standalone novel with my personal guarantee of a magical happily ever after!

"The chemistry in this is off the charts hot!"
Goodreads reviewer

Wolf Stone, no matter how drop-dead gorgeous he was, was out of his freaking mind. And an asshole to boot. "You left Nate out there?" Kayla Fagan demanded. "Have you seen the weather?"

"He's not made of sugar."

"If this is how you treat your fellow operatives, what do you do to your enemies?"

He shrugged. "None of them left alive to tell." He smiled, and it did nothing to soften his features. The quick curve was more wicked than anything, making his eyes darken, reminding her of those few moments of twilight before the sky devoured the sun.

He strode from the kitchen, and she followed. "Mr. Stone—"

"Wolf, or just Stone." He didn't slow down. "And I'm not worried about how I'll sleep tonight." He crouched in front of the hearth, tossing kindling into the empty fireplace grate.

Even though she was stunned by his bad behavior, she couldn't help her fascination as she watched him. His shoulders were impossibly broad. Long black hair, as wild as he was, was cinched back with a thin strip of leather. And Lord, he had the hottest ass she'd ever seen.

Thunder cracked, and she worried about Nate. "I

think you should at least invite him in until the storm passes." Even though it was summer, weather could be extreme at this elevation.

"Save your breath." Stone struck a match, filling the room with the sharpness of sulfur. "My mind is made up."

"You can have a heart, just until the weather clears. Then you can go back to your regularly scheduled…" She stopped short of saying assholeishness. "Grumpiness."

His mouth was set, brooking no argument. "Let it be."

Huge splatters of rain hit the floor-to-ceiling windowpanes.

Wolf might be able to sleep at night if he left his comrade out there, but she would toss and turn with worry.

Decision made, Kayla crossed to the hallway closet, pulled open the gigantic golden oak doors, and took out a raincoat. She also grabbed her gun and checked it before tucking it into her waistband. She snatched up a pair of compact binoculars and a compass and was shoving her arms in the sleeves of the yellow slicker as she walked through the great room on the way to the back door.

"What do you think you're doing?"

"Exactly what you said. I'm saving my breath." Kayla

spared him a glance. "I decided not to argue with you."

"Stop right there."

He spoke softly, but his voice snapped with whiplash force. Despite herself, she froze. She'd faced untold danger, but this man, unarmed, unnerved her. A funny little knot formed in the pit of her stomach.

Kindling crackled as fire gnawed its edges.

"Turn around." His voice was terrifying in its quietness. "Look at me, Fagan."

Struggling not to show the way she was trembling, she turned.

He stood. "I will be very clear, Ms. Fagan. You are here at my pleasure." He took a single step toward her. "I will not be disobeyed."

His statement was loaded with threat.

Wildly she thought of the room in the basement, the one with crops and paddles hanging from the walls. The one she'd been forbidden to enter, and the door she'd opened the first time he'd left the house.

She locked her knees so she didn't waver. "I've never been much for obedience."

"Nathaniel Davidson is far from helpless."

"He's a fellow member of the team." She pivoted and walked away.

The wind whipped at the door, nearly snatching it from her hand.

She turned up the collar of her ineffective raincoat.

There was never anything friendly about a Rocky Mountain storm.

Fortunately, she didn't have far to trudge. In less than fifteen minutes, the ground beneath her sizzling with electrical ferociousness, she saw a streak of orange.

She grinned.

Members of her team were smart. Nate had donned a reflective safety vest. That would, at least, stop friendly fire.

"Davidson!" When she got no response, she called out a second time.

He started toward her. "Come to rescue me, have you?" he shouted above the roar of the wind. "Bet Stone told you to come."

"He sends his regards and invites you to sit next to the fire while he pours you a cognac."

Nate laughed. "How much trouble are you in for coming after me?"

"He didn't threaten to flay the skin from my hide."

"Doesn't mean he won't."

"Thanks. That's a comforting thought."

Thunder crashed.

"I ought to write both of you up."

Wolf. Her breath threatened to choke her. How much had he overheard? It shouldn't have surprised her that he'd followed, that he'd effortlessly covered the same ground she had in far less time. The man was in shape, and he kept himself sharp, the same way he had when he led American troops in the Middle East.

Over the lash of the summer storm, his voice laden with command, he said, "Both of you, back to the house."

The wind snatched a few strands of hair and whipped them against cheekbones that could have been sculptured from granite. His jaw was set in an uncompromising line. Out here, in the unforgiving elements, he appeared even more formidable than he had in the house.

Nate glanced at her. "Maybe I will get a cognac after all."

"No fucking chance," Stone fired back.

Cheerfully, as if he couldn't have been happier, Nate whistled and gamely started down the mountainside. No one should be happy about this kind of reception.

"Move it, Fagan," Stone instructed, leaning forward so he could issue his command directly into her ear.

"Yes, sir."

Steps short but sure, she followed Nate, leaving Stone to bring up the rear.

Minutes later, the mean-looking sky unleashed a torrent. Earth became mud. Rocks became as slick as ice.

She lost her balance, and Stone was there, wrapping an arm around her waist, pulling her up and back, flush against the solidness of his body.

The sensation zinging through her was from him,

not the streak of lightning. "I'm good. Fine."

He held her for a couple of seconds, his warm breath fanning across her ear. What would happen if she leaned back for just a bit longer and allowed herself to be protected in his strong arms? To feel his cock against her? To surrender to the fantasies that kept her awake at night and her pussy damp, even now?

And what fantasies they were.

Last night's sight of his semierect dick had driven her mad.

After he returned to his own room, she'd thought of the crops and paddles in his downstairs room. She'd pictured him using them on her while she gasped and strained, and ultimately surrendered to the inevitable. Turned on and needy, she'd pulled up her sleep shirt and parted her labia to find her clit already hardened.

She'd come with a quiet little mew and wanted nothing more than to scream the house down as his cock pounded her.

What was wrong with her? She couldn't afford thoughts like this with any man, particularly one she was sent to protect. Because of the risk inherent in working for Hawkeye Security, many employees were fueled by adrenaline, and affairs were common. But everyone knew the rules. No commitments. No emotions were allowed to get in the way of the job. But the way he held her was an invitation she wanted to accept.

When he released her, a chill crept under her jacket. This time, being more careful, she followed Nate's path.

The trip up had taken maybe about fifteen minutes. Down took half an hour. And by the time they reached the home's patio with its outdoor kitchen and oversize hot tub, the sky was spitting out pieces of ice in the form of hail.

Very polite country, this.

Minding her manners, she took off her shoes and left them on a rubber mat, then hung the slicker on a peg.

Kayla told herself two lies. First, that she wasn't stalling. Second, that her fingers were shaking because of the cold weather.

Stone unlocked the back door and indicated she should precede both men into the kitchen.

Nate followed her, and then Stone relocked the door behind them.

"You." Stone pointed a finger at Nate. "What the hell were you thinking?"

Nate took a step back for self-preservation.

Both men dripped water and tracked mud. Neither seemed to care. And neither seemed to notice she was even there.

"You knew I wouldn't invite you here."

Nate shrugged. "You don't want anyone. Because you're a fool."

"A *fool*?"

"For always thinking you can do it alone. And you damn well know it."

The men were a study in contrast. Fair to dark. Alpha to beta.

"Fuck your ego, Stone. There's no place I'd rather be." Nate's tone was flat, as if that explained everything.

Kayla sucked in a breath when Wolf devoured the distance to pin Nate against the counter. Nowhere to run. Nowhere to hide.

"Wolf," she said, licking her lower lip.

"You." He shot Kayla a frightening glance. "I will deal with you directly."

Her stomach plummeted to her toes. She was watching two magnificent warriors spar, and if she wasn't careful, she'd be collateral damage.

To find out more about Nate and Kayla, check out
Come To Me HERE.

www.sierracartwright.com/hawkeye/come-to-me

All Hawkeye books are standalones
with a happily ever after!

OTHER TITLES BY SIERRA CARTWRIGHT

Titans
Sexiest Billionaire
Billionaire's Matchmaker
Billionaire's Christmas

Hawkeye Series
Come To Me
Trust In Me
Meant For Me

Bonds
Crave
Claim
Command

The Donovans
Bind
Brand
Boss

Mastered
With This Collar
On His Terms
Over The Line
In His Cuffs
For The Sub
In The Den

Master Class
Initiation
Enticement

Individual titles
Double Trouble
Shockwave
Bound and Determined
Three-Way Tie
Signed, Sealed, and Delivered
His to Claim
Hard Hand

Made in the USA
Las Vegas, NV
24 March 2021

19922665R00085